Praise for The Burqa Cave

Bravo Dean Petersen! This book pulled me into its world. The richness of the descriptions kept me reading well past my bedtime.
 —*Tiffany Howell*

Petersen has crafted a story which had me gripped from the very beginning, skillfully blending a small-town murder mystery with a ghost story. The characters were thoroughly relatable, the flashbacks and nightmares related to Tim's PTSD believable, and the plot is completely engrossing. *The Burqa Cave* is an excellent read, both for fans of murder mysteries as well as fans of horror and the supernatural. A solid 5 stars.
 —*P.J. Blakey-Novis*

The Burqa Cave weaves a haunting tale of desperate isolation, fear, and a budding trust that will stay with you after the last page has been read.
 —*Jeana Byrne*

If you enjoy horror stories that will keep you scared and turning the page, then *The Burqa Cave* is for you. I haven't been so enthralled with a story in a long time. Definitely a story worth reading more than once. A supernatural horror story that is mixed with the real-life horrors of war.
 —*Jordan Walter*

THE BURQA CAVE

THE BURQA CAVE

by
DEAN PETERSEN

SASTRUGI PRESS
Jackson, WY

For permission requests, write to the publisher, addressed
Attention: Permissions Coordinator
Sastrugi Press, P.O. Box 1297, Jackson, WY 83001, United States.

www.sastrugipress.com

Library of Congress Catalog-in-Publication Data
Library of Congress Control Number: 2019942055
Petersen, Dean
The Burqa Cave / Dean Petersen- 1st United States edition
p. cm.
1. Murder 2. Mystery 3. Paranormal

Summary: Still haunted by Iraq, a retired soldier seeks solace teaching high
school in Wyoming. He soon finds the quiet town is home to murders, mani-
acs, and a boy who can see where missing murder victims are.

ISBN-13: 978-1-944986-71-1 (hardback)
ISBN-13: 978-1-944986-72-8 (paperback)

Sastrugi Press
00139

Printed in the United States of America when purchased in the United States

10 9 8 7 6 5 4 3 2 1

For my son Clayton

CHAPTER 1

They said there was a body out there. Somewhere in the gray clay hills, past the gleaming shell casings of .22's lying in the dust, beyond the farthest landing of a bottle rocket's pink rudder. Her corpse was rumored to be somewhere in the narrow canyons that twisted into a cobwebbed maze of crumbling peaks and eroding ravines.

Tim stared down at the sun-baked carcass of an antelope, its skin pulled taut over a gaunt frame now void of guts or meat. Just bleached bones and fur. The hair coming off in tufts from its leather jerky skeleton.

At over seven thousand feet above sea level, there was little atmosphere to resist the piercing white light of an August sun reflecting off the clay.

It started, like a lot of memories, at the tip of Tim's nose. A tingling electric sensation that swelled over him like a heat wave. A momentary lapse of time and space, a single teardrop of sweat that rolled out of an armpit over his ribs and made him feel like he was there again. He had hidden from it so well, in a place of snow and rain and subzero temperatures, the occasional short story, the cautious bottle of beer, lots of football on ESPN —they had all helped him keep it at bay. But now, during this scorching summer, the heat had caught up with him and the alabaster-bleached landscape had taken him back to the place he had been running from ever since he had left it.

A burning sun cut through a different blue sky. Someone was screaming, an awful high-pitched wailing, babbling he didn't understand. He could feel the heat on his skin, the awful gritty tightness of his body under the sweat-stained Kevlar.

The bisected frame of a young child, the bottom half of its corpse literally vaporized, its intestines flopping limply and loosely like nightcrawlers from the maw above where its hips had been. The smell of cordite, of burning rubber, the awful unending stink of filth and diesel and heat.

Tim remembered the dull thud of his rifle's muzzle against the woman's sternum. He felt guilty about that still. Hitting her there was probably what triggered it. She surged at him again, still clutching the slithering viscera of her child. He hit her in the chest with the rifle's tip once more as she screamed and thrust what had been her baby at him.

"Get back!" he yelled at her.

She did not stop pushing the dead child at him.

"Get back!" he repeated, thrusting his weapon forward and hoping he wouldn't have to raise it to his shoulder and align its sights on her as he'd done before seeing the crumpled, bloody horror in her arms.

Their medic was already busy scrambling over their own guys who'd been hit by the blast. Tim's muscles tensed as he glanced around at the disaster surrounding him. Now, in the midst of chaos, his mind reached out to the thread of instruction they had given him a world away about "360 security" and "cordoning." He needed to secure the perimeter and make order out of all this. Flames billowed from the blackened skeleton of what had been one of the countless Iraqi econo-cars, now turned into a smoking husk of burning petroleum and upholstery.

The child's intestines flopped against his exposed wrist as the woman thrust the corpse at him. They left a sticky warm spot amid the pale flesh and blond hairs of his arm. Tim turned back in surprise and found himself looking into the woman's face. Her eyes were black, tear-stained and desperate.

For a long moment they stared at one another amid the yelling and the roaring flames.

She held up the baby and thrust it at him once more. What he saw had him draw his weapon to his shoulder and point its sights at her forehead.

***

Tim woke up in the cramped bedroom, sucking air into his lungs as he tried to breathe. He gasped the way a diver does when finally reaching the surface after nearly drowning.

It wasn't the first time. He knew he had a myriad of symptoms, most of which he tried to ignore—nightmares, uneasiness, easily startled by noises. Even odors and things he touched could trigger memories. They had called it shell shock in the First World War. Tim had read that even Civil War veterans passing their last years in mental hospitals had proudly displayed their medals on their nightgowns and wheeled themselves out for formations that no one came to inspect.

I don't have it that bad, he told himself. *I can still deal.*

Settling back on the sweaty sheets, he tried to control his breathing.

In out, in out. That's what they taught him at the VA. Focus on your breathing.

You're going to make it.

The phrase almost triggered another memory, but Tim closed his eyes and fought against it. He could feel the air going into his lungs and life seeping back into his bloodstream.

You're here, he told himself. *You're safe.*

He opened his eyes and looked up at the sagging acoustic-tiled ceiling. It occurred to him that homes and bases in Iraq weren't built with old asbestos tiles from 1950.

Tim rolled out of bed and lowered his feet to the green shag carpet, running them back and forth and feeling the dirty fibers brushing against his callused heels.

The sun bore through the cracked window sash like a laser pointer. It projected a bright yellow-orange pinprick, a warning of just how hot and trigger-laden the day would be.

Lacing up his Asics, he ran out the back door to the swollen river that coursed through the tiny town. Running was a ritual that demanded eight miles every day, rain, snow, or shine, or the demons would come to visit him. As long as he was moving fast, putting in all his effort, he could be what he thought he was supposed to be. Strong, determined, a self-assured warrior, who still knew exactly what to do in any situation. Not someone who was wounded and drifting. If he ran fast enough, none of his past, none of himself or what he had done, would be able to catch up with him.

After accepting a teaching job and moving to Meadowlark, Wyoming from Phoenix, he had told a friend on the phone, "It's like a third-world country, but everyone's white." What he had meant was that, like some underdeveloped nation, no one seemed to be in too much of a hurry. It took forever for his appliances to be delivered, and to buy anything beyond groceries meant a forty-five minute drive east or west just to get to a Wal-Mart.

In the teachers' lounge, on his first day, an old man who had seemed to be made entirely of bone and polyester, shambled up to him sporting a pearl-button cowboy shirt and Wrangler slacks.

"I'm Eldon Carson," the old man had said amicably, holding out his right hand while the left toted a bottle of orange juice. "I'm the guidance counselor."

Tim had met lots of shrinks. Civilian ones, military ones,

chaplains with degrees in counseling. However, he'd never met one who looked like he could change a tire. Not until this aged cowboy sat next to him. His handshake was like sandpaper. Amid the tangle of knuckles and split fingernails, Tim spied the missing tip of an index finger.

The usual line of questioning had ensued about where Tim came from and what had brought him out there. Tim had answered them all pretty honestly, but had managed to say nothing about Iraq or what had really brought him to Wyoming.

"I think you're the kind of fella who'll like a place like Meadowlark," the old man had said.

"I hope so."

"Quiet, no commotions, no tall buildings or folks running around with strange agendas. It was the best place for me after I got back."

"Got back?"

The old man smiled at him before standing up. "The only thing harder than being out there was coming back." He had swatted Tim on the shoulder before throwing his empty orange juice bottle in the trash on his way out the door.

Hearing the old man list everything Tim feared and hated, tall buildings that could hide snipers, the overall fear of noise and "commotions" had almost brought the terror of Iraq right into that teachers' lounge in Meadowlark. Had the old man already heard Tim's story through gossip, or did Tim have a tell of some kind? Was he weird in some way that told people he was PTSD incarnate, or was it just the good/bad way Vets sometimes recognized things in other Vets?

Now, running by the river that flowed through Meadowlark, Tim wondered why the usual assortment of fishermen weren't there on its banks. David Jenkins appeared at the usual spot where the river curved by the trailer that the boy lived in. For the past three weeks, the lonely teenager had started running with Tim. This had freaked Tim out a little bit at first. A single man becoming involved with a teenager might be met with suspicion even in a place like Meadowlark, where people still seemed as trusting and friendly as caricatures from the 1950s. Initially, he just waved at David when the boy appeared at his spot by the river and then casually sped up, certain he would lose him in the next quarter mile.

The thing was, despite everything else that was wrong with the gangly, awkward kid, David made a very good distance runner. All legs, with no body fat. The skeletal boy could keep up with him for the full 3.7 miles from his house to where the pavement ended and back.

On the first day of school the previous fall, when the fourteen-year-old had parked his wiry frame in Tim's Freshman English class, he had been wearing light blue running shorts that made his already freakishly long legs appear even longer and a gray t-shirt with the presidents' heads sprouting from Mount Rushmore. To top it off, he wore ugly wire-frame glasses that were too big for his face. His dry, dandruffy hair hung unkempt over his zit-covered brow.

David was the kind of kid people noticed, but not in a good way. He reminded Tim of other weird kids he had known who couldn't have fitted in even if they had tried. They were tall skinny boys who were fond of sci-fi novels, which they read antisocially wherever they went. They still played with Ninja Turtles in the lonely darkness of their bedrooms.

A lot of the self-appointed nerds Tim had encountered were lazy and hid behind a guise of self-proclaimed genius to avoid working. David, however, had put in a real effort in Tim's class. Just before the school year ended, the teenager had turned in a short story for extra credit.

Sitting in front of the TV on Friday night near the end of the school year, Tim picked up David's offering, red-tipped pen in hand, dismayed at the thought that he would probably have to wade through a bunch of crap about elves and space travel. His class in Arizona had produced plenty of *Lord of the Rings* rip-offs and they were always written by gangly virgins like David.

What Tim read made a complete break from the norm. "Jennifer" was the story of a young man living in a trailer with an odd assortment of relatives. Trying to fit in with a group of jocks, he witnessed them murder a mentally handicapped girl and bury her body in the hills outside town.

The Monday before school ended for the year, Tim handed the story back to David with a score of ninety-five percent and the phrase "good job—talk to me after class" written at the top.

Tim had no problem with violence, some profanity, even some non-graphic sexual elements appearing in the kids' stories as long as there were realistic consequences to actions. It got them interested in writing. But David's story had cut too close to home after a recent tragedy the town still struggled to understand.

After the bell rang, David arrived obediently in front of Tim's desk, peering at him from behind his huge glasses.

"Hey, Dave," Tim said, trying to sound as casual as possible. "Grab a chair." He pointed to the plastic green chair by his desk. "How you doin'?" he asked as the boy sat down.

"Good," said the boy shyly.

"Cool. What are you going to do this summer?"

"Uh… mostly hang out," he replied, looking down at his closed hands.

"Cool," Tim responded, realizing small talk wasn't going to get him anywhere with this kid. "You've done a really good job this year and I enjoyed that story you wrote."

The boy continued to stare at his hands.

"It freaked me out a bit. Where did you get the idea for it?"

The teen slowly looked up. "Jennifer?"

"Yeah, Jennifer."

"Well…" David began, "you've heard about her, right?" His squeaky voice hummed in his sinuses.

"No."

"They say some guys raped her and killed her out by the gun range. They say she's still buried out there."

"When did this happen?" Tim asked.

"In the eighties or something."

"So people just talk about it, then?"

"Yeah."

"I wondered if maybe it had something to do with what's happened."

The kid shook his head.

"Two other students have written extra credit stories about girls going missing or being… *hurt*," he said, not feeling able to use the exact words for what had really happened to the girl who used to sit just a few chairs away from Tim's desk. "I think their stories were just ways of dealing with what happened, but yours was so… vivid, so detailed… I just thought we should talk since it's similar."

"It isn't the same story, Mr. Ross."

"Right, it wasn't the same story. It's just that…" Tim found himself casting an eye over the columns of empty desks back to where Heather Brady had sat before she became the victim of the "worst crime in south west Wyoming since the seventies."

"How'd you come up with it?"

The boy sighed. "Everyone sees stuff they don't like."

Tim stared at him, waiting for him to elaborate, but the only response was, "You know I'm going out for football?"

"Uh-huh," Tim said, nodding and trying not to imagine the stork-like legs of the boy snapping in a low tackle. He couldn't help feeling it wasn't anything to brag about. Almost every kid who showed up for the school's tiny team made at least a JV spot.

"Well, it's a tradition that every year before school is out the team takes all the new guys out there at night to look for Jennifer out there at the range."

"You go try to dig her up?" Tim asked, wondering at the surreal image of letterman-jacketed kids prowling through the dark with pickaxes and shovels, like some latter-day prospectors.

"No, we just went out there and built a bonfire and then one of the varsity guys told us the story of Jennifer."

"Sounds like wholesome entertainment," Tim frowned. Did any of these kids understand just how insensitive a ritual like that might be in the wake of what had happened only a few months before?

"Then they poured water onto the fire and we were supposed to see her in the smoke."

"Bloody Mary," Tim said.

"What?"

"When I was a kid people—mostly girls—would flash the overhead lights on and off in the bathroom and see the image of a woman called Bloody Mary in the mirror. You haven't heard of that?" Tim asked, surprised.

David remained blank-faced.

"It was kind of like what you're talking about."

"After you see Jennifer it's supposed to help bond the team together or something," David said, his eyes searching Tim's own for the logic in it.

"So, did you see her?" Tim asked, goading the boy and expecting to hear a wild tale of how the twisting smoke of the extinguished fire in the low light "sorta—kinda looked like a lady's face."

Instead, the boy stared at his feet. "After Kent Larson put the fire out everyone was trying to see her when a bunch of cars and trucks came tearing out to the range and the varsity guys showed up and started chasing us around with super-soakers filled with cow pee. I took off."

"I would, too."

"I ran so far away that when they stopped and started laughing and welcoming everyone onto the team, I was too embarrassed to climb down out of the cliffs and have them see how scared I got. Then my ride left without me."

"You were out there alone?" Tim asked, knowing he wouldn't want to be on that secluded range at night by himself, regardless of any campfire theatrics.

The boy nodded.

"Sounds like you were the bravest one. I wouldn't want to be out there!" He hoped to bolster the kid's confidence a little.

David didn't respond to the flattery. Instead, he looked off into the corner of the room. The sound of kids running and yelling outside the window penetrated the silence for a moment, then Tim started to grow annoyed.

"You all right?"

The boy nodded slowly, still avoiding eye contact. "Do you... think that ghosts are real, Mr. Ross?"

"No, I don't think so," Tim answered, curious why the boy wanted to know. "Do you?"

The teen pulled his gaze from the corner and studied his teacher for a moment. Tim had seen fear before. Not the good-natured, slumber party jump-out-and-say-boo fear. This was the real thing, the wide-eyed, alabaster-complexion pall that fell over men and boys' faces when gunfire and blood and explosions bore witness to them that they were never going home. He didn't expect to see the same face on a fourteen-year-old boy in Meadowlark, Wyoming though.

"You all right?" Tim repeated.

Staring into David's eyes he could almost see the same light blue eyes of a private he had known, face white with fear, hands wrapped around a tiny crucifix in the darkness of an old house rocking with incoming mortars. In the nick of time, Tim tore his gaze away and took a breath, reassuring himself that he was still back home in a room that hummed with air conditioning and the faint whiff of cafeteria lasagna.

You've made it all year without one screw-up. Be cool.

Tim felt the room's air-conditioned chill go down the back of his throat and into his lungs. He exhaled before hazarding a glance at the scared kid again.

David Jenkin's wide-eyed terror had thankfully passed. Instead, the odd boy's expression had changed to a look of concern.

"*You* okay, Mr. Ross?"

"Yeah," Tim replied, trying to keep his voice even.

The boy continued to examine him with the same worried look and that bothered Tim.

"I just don't feel real good," he said gruffly.

The boy knew he was being lied to, but took the opportunity to change the subject.

"Do I have to rewrite the story or something?"

"No, bud," Tim told him, thankful that his voice began returning to normal. "Just wanted to make sure everything was... okay, you know? Are you sure there's nothing else on your mind?"

After a long pause, the boy shook his head.

"You have a yearbook?" Tim asked, hoping to change gear.

"Nah, I don't have the money."

Tim felt bad for him. "They're overrated anyway."

The boy eventually schlepped out of his chair and left.

Now that David had started to haunt Tim on his morning runs, he was forced to remember that odd exchange in his classroom. Tim had considered changing his route, but found there were only so many places you could run to in such a small town, and he liked his river route the best even if it did go by David's trailer.

They reached the end of the blacktop where another three-tenths of a mile would take them up a dirt road to the gun range where the football players' idiotic theatrics had scared the kid beyond what was probably appropriate. The rounded clay hills of the gun range confined the contours of the Meadowlark Valley. Mostly gray and lifeless as the moon, their steep slopes bore thin pastel pink bands left by the receding waters of a Cretaceous sea. Locals called the maze of twisted canyons and dry washes peppered with trilobites and shale "the badlands."

Tim shot a glance at David, studying his expression as they neared the lunar ridges and spurs that reached out towards them like the arms of monsters.

The boy's eyes seemed fixed on a far-off spot.

At the end of the blacktop, the two runners turned in the other direction and headed back towards town. Again Tim tried to read David's expression to see if he would make a telltale glance back in the direction of the gun range, but his eyes picked a new point on the horizon as he bounded forward.

Tim had thought about talking to Al Buoncuore, the athletics director, or maybe even the principal, about what had happened. Mentioning that perhaps using the fictional or real rape and murder of a woman didn't need to be a bonding experience for teenage kids, especially after what had happened to one of the students so recently. But then he felt less sure it was a good idea.

What would he say? That David Jenkins appeared really "upset" by what had happened? Jenkins wasn't the kind of kid that people would buck a trend for. He wasn't popular or looked up to and he didn't have the kind of last name that inspired deference around town. He was poor and lived "back in with all that trailer trash." Tim didn't believe someone like Buoncuore would keep the kid's fear a secret, let alone do anything to stop what had been going on.

The sun glistened off the fresh blacktop of the resurfaced road, almost making it look like the asphalt itself was sweating. The heat radiated up from the paved shoulder and through the soles of their running shoes, burning the bottoms of their feet.

Tim couldn't put his finger on it exactly, but he could tell that something had been left out when he and the boy had talked. He had known it since that last week of school, and in a summer all too free of convenient distractions he couldn't let it go anymore.

"Dave..." he began as they reached the spot near the trailer where the boy usually deserted him.

"Yeah?"

Tim looked down at the morning sun flashing off the rapids in the river, still not totally sure if he would be able to get the kid to talk about what had happened. "You want to get a burger?"

"I don't have any money."

"I'll get it," Tim said, veering onto the path towards his own house, "I'll meet you in an hour at the drive-in."

CHAPTER 2

Tim went home, showered, and then rode his bicycle to the only burger place in town. Fading blue plastic letters in Old English script read, "Chuck's Drive-In," above the shake-shingle roof reminiscent of an aged Pizza Hut or Waffle House. At least twice a week Tim craved the thick, all-beef patties formed in the mysterious recesses behind Chuck's little window, where anonymous hands placed food on a ledge and dinged a bell. Given that the place didn't look to have had a renovation since the seventies, he could almost believe that consuming fat and cholesterol inside this virtual time machine would somehow revert the damage he was doing to himself and take him back to a time before the invention of vegans, whole food and clean eating.

Parking his bike alongside the building, he half hoped David wouldn't be there, but he found the kid waiting in the shade by the front door, absently gazing at a line of dead grass wilting in a crack in the asphalt.

"You hungry?" Tim asked as he opened the door and led the boy into a noisily air-conditioned lobby flanked by faux wood panels and bright orange booths that would have made the Brady Bunch proud.

Tim ordered a double cheeseburger and a chocolate milkshake with a peanut butter swirl. David only asked for a corn dog.

Seated at a chipped Formica table, Tim watched the kid pick disinterestedly at his food. At ten thirty-seven in the morning they were the only customers.

"You a gamer?" Tim asked, remembering that conversation

with this odd boy wasn't going to be easy and that this whole thing had probably been a dumb idea.

"Yeah."

"What ones?"

"I used to like *World of Warcraft*, but now I've started to play *Call of Duty* a lot."

"I used to play that one."

Tim didn't want to say why he no longer played it, but David suddenly seemed to start reading between the lines.

"Kids at school said you went to... Afghanistan?"

Tim frowned and looked out the window as an obese, brown lab with dusty fur padded through the heatwaves from the burning asphalt. It curled into the shadow of the burger place as if it owned that particular spot under the eaves.

"Iraq," Tim corrected, dreading what else his students might have said. He had never talked about it with any of them. He had even removed a picture he used to keep on his desk of his squad glaring into the camera in front of an Iraqi palace after the kids kept asking lurid questions about it.

"Did you kill anybody?" the boy asked.

Tim shot a look of surprise. David stared back through two Coke bottle lenses with a mantis-like lack of emotion. Tim transferred his gaze to the window and the fat dog outside before answering.

"A lot of people died there, Dave."

Tim could feel David's bug-like eyes on him as he watched the dog panting in the shade. It was weird that even David, who normally seemed to dwell in a world of his own, could tell that Tim was not being forthcoming about his own terrible experiences either.

"I'm sorry," David said quietly.

Tim looked at the boy, whose attention had returned to his

corn dog and noted the contrition in his expression.

"You don't need to be."

Tim wondered if he had somehow hurt the feelings of this normally aloof, strange kid. He looked around at the empty booths, half wanting to tell David something honest and real about Iraq as a concession. A banner on the far wall bore the high school's mascot, with the phrase "Chuck Supports Our Screaming Meadlowlarks" underneath.

"You excited about football this fall?" he asked. "I don't think that stupid initiation thing will matter if you want to play."

"I don't want to do it anymore," David told him.

"I don't blame you," Tim said.

"Did you ever run cross-country?" The kid asked.

"Yeah, Freshman year before I could make weight for football."

The boy looked surprised.

"I used to be really small and skinny until the summer I turned fifteen," Tim explained.

"I saw Mr. Buoncuore at the grocery store a few days ago and he said if I can get three guys who want to run and a teacher who'll say he's our coach, then the school will have a team."

"Just three?" Tim asked. It still amazed him how small the schools were in rural Wyoming and how tiny the sports teams were. "Is that why you've been running with me?"

David shrugged. He picked up his corn dog and took his first real bite of lunch.

"I'll talk with Buoncuore about coaching," Tim heard himself say because he figured that was what this strange, lonely boy wanted. "Can you find three other guys who would want to run?" He hoped the skepticism he felt about the boy having many friends didn't show in his voice.

"I think so."

Tim had never coached kids before, but he figured that it would mostly consist of telling a bunch of scrawny youth to "Keep going!" and "Run faster" for a few miles every day after school.

"I guess it'd be good for the kids at school to have something to do if they don't play football this fall," Tim added, trying to convince himself that he didn't mind helping out.

The boy stared out the window at the dog, which had rolled onto its side and closed its eyes for a nap.

"Maybe you guys could come up with your own initiation ritual," Tim joked, hoping to make the kid laugh.

David stared at Tim with a hint of the same wide-eyed fear he'd revealed when they had talked last.

"Or not!" Tim added hastily, looking out at the sleeping dog with self-loathing and a wish that he could just close his eyes and sleep like that dog for the rest of the roasting summer.

They ate in silence for a minute or more.

"Dave," Tim began, hoping that this awkward lunch he'd inflicted on them both wouldn't suddenly be made worse by making the kid re-live some traumatic event that might cause him to flip out in the middle of Chuck's dining room, "you sure something more didn't happen at that gun range?"

The boy swallowed and Tim watched the lump travel down his skinny throat.

"'Cause if it did, I'll listen to whatever is on your mind."

David rolled his lips between his teeth without looking up from his meal. "You said you don't believe in ghosts?"

Tim shrugged. "No... not really, but I'll believe whatever you tell me," he offered, feeling a little corny after saying it.

Still eyeballing his food, David took a long breath as if bracing for something.

"You can tell me."

The boy didn't look up.

"Nothing happened," he murmured hollowly.

David stood and, keeping his eyes on his meal tray, slid it off the table and dumped its contents into the trash. Tim heard the clatter of the cowbell above the door as the boy left. He watched David through the window taking off in a loping run across the asphalt.

CHAPTER 3

Tim felt the crystals of salty alkali crunching like frost-encrusted brambles under the worn tread of his combat boots. Now starched with salt and sweat, the fabric of his uniform felt like a baked potato skin intent on sucking up all the heat of the world as he trudged over the white-hot clay.

The pistol grip of his army-issued M-16 swung with each step between his thumb and index finger. Always ready, his best friend, his girlfriend, his mother and his pet dog Pumpkin all rolled into one—a 39.5 inch, 8.79 pound "little friend" that could be drawn up to its happy spot on his shoulder in less than a quarter of a second and annihilate, destroy, kill anything that threatened the chance of him going home alive. It felt so good to have it dangling there, swinging like a death-dealing pendulum between thumb and forefinger.

Tim's gaze switched from near to far, left to right as he checked every crag and ridge for the silhouette of anything human—the telltale head and shoulders of a man jutting from the top of outcroppings or above the walls of the narrow canyon, the glint of sunlight off anything metallic, anything unnatural. The stifling heat inside his crusted uniform stirred the ghost of an old but pleasant memory, a vague reminder of a very faraway place where his mother handed him his jeans fresh out of the dryer on a December morning, enclosed in their warmth on the slow bus ride to school.

The Kevlar of his helmet was almost hot enough to burn the tops of his ears off. A drop of sweat the size of a baby's pinky nail sprouted from his scalp and ran its quicksilver course over his brow and onto an eyelash. Tim winced and shot his left hand up, digging his pointer finger under his ballistic eyewear as he tried to wipe the sweat from his burning eye.

He cursed at the salty stinging. The army had issued camel backs, automatic weapons with ACOG scopes, encrypted radios, but no one had ever issued a way to keep the sweat out of your eyes.

Rounding the bend of the sweltering ravine he realized he was alone. Although he'd never been alone "downrange" before, somehow it didn't bother him. At least, not until he passed the curve where the canyon came to a dead end and a layer of shale stretched across the chasm ahead forming a cave. He dropped to his right knee, swinging his rifle into position and drew a bead on the figure crouching in the shadows of the cavern.

About forty yards away the human form squatted in a black burqa, totally motionless except for the slight wafting of its hem in the dusty stir of a low breeze. Some women in Iraq wore burqas, but Tim had never seen one with her face completely covered before. He couldn't see the figure's eyes, but he could tell they were watching him. Women were rarely alone here, but this one had no friends or relatives at hand. He shot cautious glances to the right and left of her. No one else. Not a child nor a dog, just this personage holding eerily still in the darkness, staring out at him.

"Marhaba!" he shouted, wanting to raise his hand in greeting but fearful of releasing his weapon.

The woman didn't move or reply.

"Marhaba! Hello!" Tim shouted again.

Still no reply. Taking another cautious look around, Tim rose and slowly advanced on the figure hunched in the cave. He held his rifle in both hands but pointed it off to the side at the low ready.

The advice most soldiers had been told about Iraqi women

was to simply leave them alone—but something wasn't right.

He closed the last few yards on the woman, tense and cautious, ready to fire if he saw the tell-tale lightning movement of a hand reaching for a weapon. Standing on the threshold of the cave now, only about six feet from her, the front of his body went ice cold, not the gentle relief of friendly shade, but the prickly frostiness of a meat locker.

The figure's eyes were veiled by a gossamer black covering. It made Tim nervous that he couldn't tell what kind of expression she wore as she silently observed him.

"Marhaba," he repeated quietly, beating to death one of the half dozen Arabic words he knew.

Tim extended a cautious left hand in the air, still keeping his right on his weapon. You weren't supposed to do much in Iraq with your left hand, but there was no way he would remove his dominant hand from the trigger of his weapon.

The woman tilted her head up. The covering over her face slid down and bunched on her chest like billowing silk pulled by unseen hands. Her face was the face of all the countless corpses he had seen—a patch of expressionless, sexless, gray-green skin the color of a soiled burial shroud.

However, unlike all the dead he had seen with that pallor, this woman's eyes were expressive and sentient. She looked like a nightmare of the all-American girl next door, with blonde feathered corn-silk hair and glacial blue eyes that would have been beautiful if not for the terror in them.

She wore a pink polo shirt with the collar flipped up, sprouting from, of all things, an ugly knitted Christmas sweater. Her hands rested low in the folds of the burqa where she cradled something unseen. Tim's attention should have been fixed on what the unseen hands were doing, but instead he couldn't help looking into her eyes.

Her lips parted. No sound came out, but she mouthed the words, "help me."

Then the girl stood, the rest of her burqa falling off and down past her jeans where it pooled at her feet on the clay floor of the cave. In her arms lay the dead baby. The lifeless, drooping hank of ribs and the limp, scarecrow arms of the spaghetti-gutted child. The blue-eyed, all-American girl thrust the bloody rag doll at Tim's chest. Screaming in Arabic the exact same words, with the exact same tone as the Iraqi woman after the car bomb, she pushed and shoved it at him.

Tim raised his weapon, slamming it against her sternum, trying to push her back, though he knew it was wrong. He didn't ever want to do it again, didn't ever want to see or hear or feel that horrible thing again. But she just kept pushing and thrusting it at him and he slammed the muzzle of his rifle against her again and again until he heard the earth-jarring bang of his rifle and felt it jump in his hands.

***

Tim woke screaming with the Arabic screams reverberating through his brain.

The ceiling fan spun over the bed in the gray darkness. He inhaled a long breath and then slowly and carefully forced the air back out of his lungs. He slid across the sweat-stained sheets, pressing his back against the headboard and scanning from left to right in the night.

Closet. Ironing Board. Dresser. All in the right place—you are here, not back there!

He opened the drawer of his nightstand and reached in. His open palm brushed the gun—the only item inside. Wrapping his hand around the rubberized grip, he pulled the .357 Magnum out and held it in his fists, pointing it at the wall.

The blue light of very early dawn made the chrome-plated gun glow silver in the dark. It felt so good in his hands, this gleaming solid piece of stainless steel. The one thing he could depend on. After he came back from Iraq, there had been a brief period in which he had abhorred all things military, but it had proved fleeting. After a while, he had found himself perusing the gun shops.

Over the past year, Tim had acquired an AR-15, a Mossberg tactical shotgun, and then, after seeing a sale advertised at a sporting goods store, he had bought the .357 the day after Thanksgiving. Unlike the small caliber 9mm pistols Americans had accepted reluctantly in Iraq, this gun was rumored to pierce engine blocks. Tim could only hope that it could send the screaming demon in his dreams back to the worst parts of his past, to sleep forever.

The first time he fired the gun, he had been startled at how hard it was to control the short-barreled little pistol. It had almost scared him, but then, thud after thud, explosion after explosion, jolted through his hands and wrists and rang in his ears and he had begun to grow numb to the shock and be warmed by the thing's power.

In a world that swirled with chaos, this little piece of steel became a touchstone of concrete reality, something he could hold onto for dear life. With his back to the wall and his pistol facing outward, he could handle anything that came for him. He had decided long ago he would pump four of the gun's five bullets into whatever monster came for him out of his dreams and save the last one for himself.

Better that than be taken captive by whatever nightmare might come to life before him.

CHAPTER 4

Morning burned into the little room haunted by Tim's nightmares. It lacked fog or any of the other dew-slicked niceties of a world taking its time to wake up. He could already feel the heat radiating off the faux wood paneling at his back.

He stared down at the glint of the revolver. It looked so shiny and ready in the burning light, this friend that never slept. Carefully, he put it back in his dresser and folded his hands in his lap.

If I ever dream about something normal again, am I so far gone that even that will scare me?

He would run today, no question about it, but right now he needed to hear the pop and clatter of his AR-15 spitting fire and flicking brass as it leapt and reset like an obedient attack dog, launching a sharp little pill of white-hot metal at almost three times the speed of sound. He needed to feel the gun stock rise up against his cheek when he fired and dig its charging handle against his nostril like the weird intimacy of some rough lover. He craved its face-jarring bounce and the deafening bang. A gun almost exactly like this had begun to transform him at Fort Benning and, some time in Iraq, it had become the one thing he relied upon to keep him alive. Not his friends, not his idealistic enlistment—just that sudden violence of burning cordite and the high-focus ability to keep the sights of his weapon on the form moving in front of him. There was a malignant rapport between man and weapon that overruled all other theories or ways of being. It had kept him alive by making sure someone else was dead.

Tim went to his closet and pulled down the long black plastic case with his rifle inside as well as a small desert camo duffle bag containing his ear and eye protection, ammo, a collapsible target stand, and half-a-dozen silhouette targets that would burst bright green when shot. He loaded them all into the Subaru and pulled out of his driveway, heading for the gun range. The clay hills in the distance made him remember the horrible story David Jenkins had written about the girl being murdered out there. He imagined the boy waiting near his trailer to join him on their morning run.

As the number of houses thinned near the edge of town, Tim found himself hanging a right turn towards the poor neighborhood by the river. He really wanted nothing more than to get away and let the bang and bounce of his rifle soothe and massage away the memory of the previous night, but he knew that the image of the poor kid lingering on the jogging path waiting for him would keep invading his mind if he didn't swing by and at least give David a raincheck to run later that day.

Mining had replaced ranching in Meadowlark as it had in much of Wyoming. However, despite the mineral wealth, there were plenty of tarnished mobile homes scattered along the oil-slicked back roads throughout the county. Tim followed a nameless dirt lane along the river and finally spotted the skinny figure of his running partner standing on the high bank.

What he had really meant to do was tell the kid they weren't going running until later but, confronted by the scarecrow figure so alone and forlorn, what he heard himself say was, "You wanna go shooting?"

David eyed Tim for a moment. "I'll have to ask my sister," he said, cocking his head at an aged trailer in the distant cottonwoods.

"That's cool. I'll wait here."

The boy shot off like a jackrabbit for the trailer and Tim watched him go as he attempted to pick out the particulars of the Jenkins residence between the tree trunks. An ancient mini-bike with a rotting seat crosshatched with duct tape melted into the shin-high grass of what passed for a front lawn. There was other debris barely clearing the unruly growth that he couldn't quite make out.

As David reappeared and loped towards the Subaru, Tim wondered if this could land him into trouble with the school. Given that Jeff Williams, the science teacher, had taken a class shooting the previous fall before the hunting season "to learn about physics" Tim doubted this would be an issue.

"My sister wants to meet you real quick," David said apologetically when he reached the car.

Tim cursed quietly and took another hesitant look at the trailer, then shifted into park and turned off the engine.

Jobless after finishing college, Tim had volunteered for a group kind of like the Peace Corps, but in Alabama. They coached sports for "rural underprivileged youth" and helped them with their homework. He remembered a few home visits he had been required to make to decrepit trailers just like this one.

He exited the car and traversed the trees till he reached the unmowed grass of the front yard, scanning for the quintessential malicious dog that might be lurking nearby, preparing to charge once you got too close to run away. He pictured the kind of half-feral, mutant-junkyard hellhound that shined as some redneck boyfriend's or uncle's pride and joy. Instead, all he saw was a blue wading pool with one side caved in, its brackish black water half obscuring a smiling plastic octopus that presumably had had no idea when it was taken from Walmart's outdoor display one hopeful summer morning that it would meet a fate like this.

Following David up a rickety contrivance of graying two-by-sixes, he dreaded the familiar probability of the odors he'd smell inside—the stink of McDonald's and old tube socks, maybe the grease of a disassembled Harley engine on a Goodwill coffee table. Or perhaps the cloying funk of caged or uncaged birds, or ferrets, or bearded dragons, or whatever other white trash pets were currently in vogue.

Tim paused on what passed for a front porch as David opened the door. He briefly hoped the boy's sister would let him undergo her required examination right where he stood, but David went on in and waved a spindly arm for him to follow. Tim grimaced and stepped onto a faded chunk of linoleum that segued into an old shag carpet. Bracing himself for the smell and doing his best to breathe only through his mouth, Tim was surprised to find the interior spotless.

He hazarded a sniff and his nostrils were met with the crisp antiseptic burn of carpet deodorizer and Pine-Sol. Against expectation, the walls were void of glowing Budweiser signs or lifesize cutouts of Troy Aikman. A black and white photo of a snowstorm had been hung in a simple frame above a modest couch flanked by smaller photos. A little coffee table with potpourri stood between the couch and an off-brand flat screen. The fading vinyl and Formica had been scrubbed to a shine, despite their age.

Tim felt someone watching him and whirled to his left. He gasped as he took in glacial blue eyes and white corn-silk hair. He searched the girl's other features, hoping for the awful sense of familiarity to end there, but the shape of the nose, the curve of the jaw—every detail—was identical. The living image of the woman in his nightmare about Iraq scrutinized him from the tiny kitchen of a mobile home in Meadowlark,

Wyoming. His stomach churned and he desperately fought the impulse to run.

"Hi!" the ghoul of his dreams said, pulling a bright yellow dishwashing glove off and approaching Tim with an out-stretched hand.

Be cool, be cool.

"I'm Abbey," the girl said, giving him a slightly skeptical look that made Tim realize he wasn't succeeding in "being cool" real well.

"I'm Tim," he stammered, extending his own hand to shake hers and feeling marginally relieved that this twenty-some-thing's skin was not, he now realized, gray-green and dead like he'd seen in his nightmare.

"I'm really sorry about the mess," she said, indicating the immaculate living room.

"It looks really good," Tim countered, thankful that he could find at least one thing to say that sounded real and normal.

"I just moved back from UW," Abbey told him, her eyes dart-ing around the old trailer. "I'm sorry it's so awful. I'm trying to get it cleaned up before I start work Monday."

Tim smiled, suddenly feeling bad for her. He had met trailer girls before—older sisters, aunts, mothers. They typically had Brillo pad hair, sleeveless shirts, and badly executed tattoos that had cost more than their cars. They were women charged by reason of death, deployment or biological accident with taking care of kids in the worst circumstances. Hoping to make her feel more at ease, Tim gestured at the picture on the wall.

"Did you take that?"

"Yeah," Abbey said, still looking a little uncomfortable. "What do you think of our winters?"

"Love 'em," Tim said, glad that he could be honest about

something. "I'll never go back to Arizona."

"Most people here hate snow, but I think it's beautiful."

"You took all these?" he asked, pointing to the other photos.

"Yep." She eyed the other pictures as if still not sure about them. "I took a photography class my sophomore year. I would have majored in it, but I really wanted to do something with animals." She looked at the window and frowned. "I'm really sorry about the yard. I'm going to rip some of that crud out of here. I got home just after Mom died, but it's not like anyone kept it up anyway."

"I'm sorry," Tim said. He had no idea that David's mother had died.

Abbey studied Tim, perhaps trying to see if she could be blunt with him. Then she shrugged. "I'm not sure I am."

Tim nodded, not wanting to pry into what she meant by that.

"We're making it," she said. "Right, Dave?" She cocked her head at David, who now sat on the sofa peering at a laptop. "Anyway, David said you wanted to go shooting?"

"Yeah." Tim felt embarrassed. "I really should have thought this through a little better. Lately David has started coming with me when I go running and he was in my class last year... I teach English at the high school..." *I'm sounding like a bigger creeper with each new word*, he thought. "Anyway, this morning I'm headed to the gun range and realized he might feel left behind." The last thing this girl needed was a strange guy disrespecting what little control she had over her life by taking her little brother to go shooting. "I should have asked you first. I didn't think it through."

"It's okay," she replied earnestly. "I really appreciate your taking him running and everything. I just wanted to see who David was spending his mornings with. It's hard being a mom now to my brother." She shot a glance down at David.

Tim smiled, preferring not to say too much to this girl who remained a dead ringer for the horror he'd seen in his dreams the previous night.

"He said you were in the military? You can teach him how to be safe and all that with a gun?"

"I was," Tim told her. "It's pretty basic stuff. I really am sorry, I should have–"

"It's okay," she repeated, shaking her head and raising her fingers slightly to stop him. "I'm glad you're taking him." Then she leaned toward David on the couch and hissed a fake whisper. "I worry about him!"

"I'm all right!" David hissed a stage whisper back at his sister.

Tim noticed a rare grin had crossed David's lips as he continued to stare down at his laptop screen. Abbey cracked a smile too, apparently this was part of some inside joke.

"If you want, you can come too," Tim offered, instantly regretting that his tone sounded a little too hopeful.

Abbey smiled and held up the dishwashing glove as she slid it back on. "I'm going to finish cleaning. You'll bring him back in one piece?"

***

"You ever shot a gun before?" Tim asked distractedly as he signaled and pulled onto the traffic-less road leading out of town.

"No," the boy replied.

Tim didn't hear him. He was already trying to figure it out. Had he seen David's sister somewhere before? Maybe in one of the old team photos hanging in the halls of Meadowlark High? Or around the small town? Dreams, and especially nightmares, picked their details from some of the most random bits of information you barely noticed over the day.

At least that was what he needed to believe.

"I want to join the army," David said.

"What?"

"I want to join after I graduate."

Tim glanced across at the usually mute kid next to him.

"Do you think I could do it?"

Tim looked back at the road. "If you want to."

"No, I mean, like—do you think I could *do* it? You know, like, handle it?"

Tim laughed. "It's the easiest thing in the world." He gave the kid another look. "Everything is at sixth-grade level," he told him, parroting what everyone in the army had said. "Yeah, you can do it."

What he didn't say was *It's what comes after it's over that's hard.*

Following the winding road into the Badlands where no sagebrush or prairie grass grew, Tim eventually turned off the main road and drove over a cattle guard. It made the rumbling sound he had grown fond of since moving to Wyoming. He parked next to a tin-roofed shack riddled with bullet holes where brass shell casings glinted in the dust all around it, like a golden halo in the morning light. A missing wall on the range side of the hut looked out over an alkali flat where the bullet-pocked remains of cardboard Coors cases and splintered target stands spread out like tombstones or broken teeth.

They got out of the car under a sign tacked to the top beam of the range shelter—also riddled with bullet holes.

This Building was constructed by Troop 308 of The Boy Scouts of America. Please be respectful.

Beneath that was a list of rules about hearing protection and other things, now almost illegible thanks to pepperings of birdshot. Someone had added their own editorial in permanent marker along the bottom of the sign.

This is a gun range not a dump! No shooting TVs or computer monitors! That means you John Henderson!

Tim grinned and turned to David, but the boy looked guardedly past the rotting target stands and smashed bottles towards the surrounding hills. They seemed to rise from the mud like living things, or Jabba the Hutt—craggy mounds with spurs and drainages resembling claws or giants' fingers. These monsters had no eyes, but even Tim started to get the uncomfortable feeling that they were being watched just the same.

"Creepy, aren't they? Like the surface of the moon or something," Tim remarked, a little quieter than he had intended.

The boy said nothing and then Tim recalled again his traumatic initiation with the football team.

"C'mon!" He walked to the back of the car, hoping to break the tension, and handed David the camo bag. Then they went down range to set up some targets.

Shooting something as powerful as a .357 Magnum with a beginner was out, but the AR-15, though not ideal, would probably be okay for the boy with Tim right there to supervise. About thirty yards from the range hut Tim assembled a target stand from the PVC pipes he'd cut long ago and then drove some old tent stakes through the holes in the base.

"It's weird there's no wind here," he observed, half to himself.

The thud of his mallet on a tent stake felt like an intrusion in the sepulchral stillness. Tim paused and looked around, speculating that the clay of the surrounding hills must swallow up sound the way snow did. He glanced at the boy, who still had the same haunted expression on his face.

"You know, Dave, in a minute you're going to learn how to annihilate anything that threatens you, so you don't need to look so spooked. Okay?"

He grinned at the boy, hoping to get a smile out of him, but David just kept staring into the labyrinth of canyons beyond the targets.

At the shoot shack, Tim pulled the rifle from its container and showed it to David, explaining how to control his breathing and not jerk the trigger if he actually wanted to hit anything. He explained basic rifle safety and, after showing him how to load a magazine, kitted David out with eye and ear protection before putting on his own.

David's first rounds flew high over the target, smacking into the clay backstops in the distance and kicking up little puffs of smoky dust. Tim took the gun back and explained how to align the sights so the top of the front sight rested in the middle of the ring made by the rear sight aperture.

Surprisingly quickly, David started to hit his target.

After sending sixty rounds of .223 mostly into the target, they stopped to reload the magazines.

"Do you like my sister?" David asked, raising his voice to be heard over the earplugs as he gingerly slid a bullet into the mag with his thin, precise fingers.

Tim cleared his throat. "Yeah, Yeah I do." He had learned that with high school kids owning to a weakness usually got them off your back faster rather than denying one.

"Are you going to hook up?" the boy asked, the phrase awkward in his mouth.

"Maybe."

David smiled. It surprised Tim how happy that seemed to make him.

"Is she single?" he asked, realizing all too soon he had betrayed what he really wanted to know.

"Yeah, she's single," David said offhandedly as he shoved

more rounds into the magazine.

Tim wanted to ask more about Abbey, but he knew the more he probed the more likely David would be to tell her about his interest and the more difficult the whole thing would become.

"Where did you go with the football team?" he asked, to change the subject, casually gesturing at the maze of crags and canyons before them.

David tapped the loaded magazine on his thigh in a way that reminded Tim of the way he had seen other guys, not much older than David, do in a land of sand and heat. Tim considered changing the subject again when the boy pointed.

"Back of that canyon."

Tim frowned, regretting that he had asked.

David shoved a magazine into the rifle, put it to his shoulder and aimed at the target. He studied it for a long time, without firing.

"You really don't think there are ghosts?" he asked, still without pulling the trigger.

Tim had a fleeting image of the dismembered baby and its mother. The rifle he had pointed at them wasn't much different from the one the boy now held.

"I really hope not," he said, not wanting to believe that the woman he had killed that day might be out there wandering in the swirling heat of a desert war zone, crying and shrieking in misery for all eternity for her spaghetti-gutted baby. It had never formed as an entirely conscious thought, but somewhere in Tim's brain he worried that if there could be life after death then that woman's spirit would come for him and take her revenge when his turn to die came.

"I'm sorry, David… about… your mom," Tim said quietly, hoping that this really might be why the boy claimed to see ghosts. It could be a coping mechanism for losing her. "I wish

I'd known sooner."

"I'm not," David said, looking sideways at Tim.

"Does this... *stuff* about ghosts have anything to do with her?"

David shook his head before looking back through the rifle's sights. "No, I haven't seen *her.*"

He slowly squeezed the trigger and the rifle leapt up with a bang.

The duo took turns shooting and as Tim emptied his third magazine he had to admit that it was weird the way the boy had said that he "hadn't seen *her.*" When Tim had fired the last round and the bolt locked back to the rear he looked up from his gun.

"David, I want you to take me to where you saw whatever it was that got your hackles up."

The boy looked as if he'd been slapped.

"It'll be okay," Tim reassured him.

David shook his head.

Tim slid a fresh magazine off the plywood table and shoved it into the weapon. "Come on, Dave, if you wanna join the army you have to be able to face all kinds of awful stuff. Just show me where it happened. You'll see that there's nothing to be scared of."

Or at least maybe I'll find out what really happened out there.

Putting the rifle's tactical sling over his neck, Tim felt a hint of something from somewhere far away—the old familiar battle rattle. He walked out of the shack towards the canyon the boy had pointed to, hoping the kid would follow. He made it about ten feet from the hut when he heard the crunch of the kid's running shoes on the clay, hurrying to catch up.

"This'll be good training for you," Tim told David as they walked over the spent brass and the eroded hills with their knuckle-like folds looming nearer. "Though you'll have to walk around in the unholy heat with a lot more gear than we have."

They rounded the jutting spur of a ridge and entered the mouth of a small canyon.

"You'll have to learn to listen to every sound and look out for any sign of unnatural movement. To identify disturbances in the landscape, look for ghosts of signs that others are there, even though they refuse to show themselves."

Tim glanced back to make sure the kid followed and then quickly looked away after he saw the fear in his eyes.

"You'll know they're there. You'll hear them. You'll see what they've left behind. But until one reveals himself to you, there's nothing you can do."

As they headed deeper into the narrowing canyon the familiar feeling of war—the hated, fabled, angst-riddled combination of crushing boredom and sheer terror—was reaching out its long broken nails and slowly trailing them down Tim's neck. He could almost hear a voice whispering with hot longing breath from somewhere far away that he was needed back there and that it was waiting. It was painful, but comforting and familiar, too. It was the first time Tim had ever embraced the suck of his awful memories instead of trying to fight them off. It felt surprisingly good as at least he now faced them, armed, and with someone else.

"And while all this is going on you'll see your friends die," he continued. "You'll see husbands be left by unfaithful wives. You'll see the world forget and, after a while, you'll end up in some foreign death pit all alone, hoping you'll see the worst thing you possibly can so that at least you'll have something to fight. And when you finally do, it will scare the living piss out of you." Tim hoisted the weapon up to his shoulder and trained its sights on an imaginary enemy ahead of them.

"Mr. Ross, I don't want to go any further," David said in a high, wavering voice.

"Why not, Dave?" Tim asked, not looking back as they moved slowly towards a sharp curve in the canyon. "I promise you, buddy, whatever is around the next bend will never be worse than what I've already seen, and nothing you can't handle."

He heard the boy's reluctant footsteps still padding behind him as they reached the turn. The war goddess's fingertips stopped their playful caress and now pincered the scruff of his neck in her talons, thrusting him into the old familiar terror.

"Then what finally happens, after all that fear and horror, month after month, you start to get used to it. You even start to sorta like it, because at least you can feel *something* again. Then, when you're home, you can't feel anything anymore unless it's just as evil and nasty as what you felt down range."

Just before rounding the bend, Tim shot a look back at the shaking boy. "Okay, David, when we round this corner if you see your worst nightmare let me know, because we're going to take care of it together."

Tim clicked the safety off, raised the rifle to his cheek, and then surged forward, watching the world bob and weave in the gunsight. Once around the curve he swung his weapon hard to the right where the narrow canyon dead-ended. There was no monster. No ghost. No malevolent observer perched on the ridges above them. Just the familiar contours of a cave formed by an overhanging ledge of shale; as black inside as a tomb.

Tim's stomach twisted. Staring down into the maw of his nightmare, a creepy sense of déjà vu washed over him. He could almost feel it again—the awful electric tension of every sun-fried moment that had changed him forever.

"Mr. Ross..."

Tim hazarded a glance back at the boy's tear-streaked face.

It brought back memories of other young men he'd led into dangerous and frightening situations. Pale, sometimes teary-eyed, sometimes vomiting, they had looked gaunt as they trembled in clean new uniforms that were too big for them. They looked like scarecrows in their Dad's suits. Thin-necked and blue-eyed, and some of them were just days away from being brought back to the land of fast food and handguns feet first, in well waxed glossy black hearses.

Tim clicked the safety on and let his weapon slide on its sling down in front of his body. He stepped towards the boy, the gun's pistol grip riding loosely in its happy spot between thumb and forefinger.

"You're all right!" he said in the low tone people used to calm horses or dogs or young soldiers who had freaked out.

The boy shook his head, his expression near anguish.

"Breathe, buddy!" Tim whispered, hearing the remorse in his own voice. He snaked an arm around David's shoulder and turned him away from whatever horror he was trying to face down in the blackness of that cave.

CHAPTER 5

As they drove back to David's house Tim felt guilty about making the boy cry. He stared at the yellow line zipping past the car and wondered why he had led David into a place so charged with terror for him in the first place.

He wanted to tell himself that it had been to show him that there was nothing to be afraid of. But there was something else. Something familiar and awful, but darkly comfortable, too. Something about the way the rifle stock and charging handle kissed his face so perfectly, even in the worst chaos of war—the way you could look through the sights of a weapon walking through the Valley of the Shadow of Death and have all your circumstances, all your concerns and worries, life's dangling participles, burn away as you focused only on shooting first and best at whatever ailed you.

Tim glanced at the broomstick-limbed boy in the passenger seat. Life had been so much easier in some ways in a war nearly seven thousand miles away than it was here.

"I'm sorry," Tim said.

David shrugged. "I'm okay."

"I shouldn't have dragged you there."

The kid bit the inside of his cheek and looked down at his running shoes. "You didn't drag me, but if it's all right I really don't want to go back there."

"We won't!" Tim insisted. "I really am sorry."

"It's not a big deal, Mr. Ross."

Tim shook his head. "I shouldn't have... scared you."

"*You* aren't what scared me."

Tim transferred his gaze from the road and saw the kid's

normally unrevealing eyes more expressive and honest than he had seen before.

"What scared you, then?"

David shook his head. "If I tell you will you believe me?"

"Yeah," Tim nodded, feeling surprisingly sincere with the kid. "Yeah, I'll try."

David took a breath and looked through the windshield. "I saw someone in that cave who looked like my sister, but all gross and rotting like a zombie. I saw her there that night when I went with the football team, too."

***

Bunch of crap! Tim thought as he shot his hands into the water like karate strikes, pulling himself through the chlorine pit of the deserted high school pool. *Just a random coincidence! A shared psychosis—isn't that what it's called?*

He reached the edge of the pool and turned, kicking off the wall to start another twenty-five meters in the other direction. He had never got the breathing down well enough to swim the right way. Instead he would turn like a drifting car when he neared the edge of the water and kick off the concrete wall.

David just lost his mother, so he now has a morbid fear of losing his other close relative. It comes out in hallucinations of seeing his sister dead, too.

Turn. Kick off the wall. Stroke! Stroke! Stroke!

Somehow my regular nightmare has turned into a pretty blonde with corn-silk hair—probably just because I've seen her around town or something. Who could blame me for having someone who looked like her locked into my subconscious?

Wall. Turn. Kick! Go!

You should have been a shrink.

Amid his frenzied strokes, Tim could almost believe it. No ghosts, or life after death, just a tragic case of rural Rocky Mountain mental illness on David's part and the ability of a coincidence to seem like something more in Tim's own paranoid brain. He didn't want to think about how much that cave just four miles away that he'd never seen before looked exactly like the one in his dream, or why he would only notice a beauty like David's sister with his subconscious and not his actual conscious if he'd seen her in passing.

Instead Tim focused his thoughts on the dilapidated trailer where he'd dropped David off just an hour before. He'd offered plenty of assurances that David would be okay and that "they would figure it all out" the next day over a burger after they had run. Who knew what kind of lead-based, meth-coated madness might be exuded by the asbestos-lined walls of David's home, despite his sister's efforts to sanitize it. The kid just needed some pills and… someone to talk to.

On reaching the far end of the pool, Tim grabbed the lip of the edge, turned and after taking a deep breath, dropped under the surface, pounding the water with everything he had. Once in a while, he would try and see how far he could go underwater before his need for air brought him up, destroying his best efforts to maintain his breaststroke and turning his progress into a mess of desperate chopping at the water and choking for air. For the moment, though, gliding beneath the surface, Tim was charmed by how everything under the surface seemed so dream-like and far away. As if the razor-thin line that divided topside from underwater was a division between worlds. Down here he felt far removed from the heat and noise and confusion that usually stalked him.

About halfway across the pool, he'd breathed out what

was left in his lungs. He did his best to become one with his blue-tinted surroundings, to ignore the growing need for air. *What if I don't go back up again? If I just keep cruising?* He imagined the world gradually closing off, like the blades of a camera aperture, until all that was left were pinpricks of light and then… black.

He pictured someone eventually finding his body resting in that blue calm underneath the black letters that said "12 ft." They would be upset, disturbed, maybe frightened as they scrambled for an aluminum pole-hook and yelled for someone to call 911, but at least he wouldn't have to feel bad anymore. He would finally be free. No more nightmares. No more visions of that terrifying woman. No more gnawing guilt that spanned an ocean and two different worlds. They would both be dead—both be even—and he could finally let go.

The concrete scraped like industrial sandpaper against his skin as he flailed an arm up and pulled himself back to the surface. Sucking in all the air in the world, it felt like being reborn or emerging from a coma.

Still clutching the edge, Tim let himself sink back into the water up to his neck as his chest heaved for air. Spidery white threads crackled like lightning across his vision, sending comets and stars across his eyes as his mind fought to return from that place he'd been contemplating. He pulled in more air and looked down at the shaking surface of the water that had almost taken him twelve feet down forever.

He pulled himself onto the deck and lay on his back. When he'd felt like this in the past he had called the Vet line. For an instant he even wondered what would happen if he called David and told him how sad, tired, and sick he really felt.

Then he frowned as he remembered how he had opened up to the kid at the range. Was he stupid? He shouldn't be talking to a kid about what it had been like back there. Though Tim had to hand it to the boy—Dave had seemed to deal with his weirdness better than most other people he had tried to open up to since coming home.

He rolled onto his knees then rose and headed to the locker room. After dressing, he went down the empty hall to his classroom and found a laminated list of phone numbers taped to the wall by the classroom's ancient beige phone. He dialed the cell phone listed next to Eldon Carson. It went through to an answering machine.

"Hey, Mr. Carson, this is Tim Ross." Tim had never been comfortable with calling the grandfatherly old man by his first name. "Listen, I know it's summer, but I'm kind of worried about David Jenkins. Skinny kid. Kinda quiet. Lives in the neighborhood over by the river? When you can, please call my cell. I just want to know if there is something that you or I can do for him. Again, I know it's summer, but... well, thanks."

Tim hung up and sat on his desk where the mid-morning sun cut a golden swathe through the dust motes that swam and tumbled in the empty classroom.

And, Mr. Carson, while you're at it, can you help me? Can you fix my nightmares and the fact that I took something from someone that I can never give back and it still eats me to death? Oh, and I sorta contemplated suicide in the school pool today. So... there's that...

He looked down at the framed photo on his desk of his Saint Bernard, Pumpkin. It occupied the space that had once been held by the picture of Tim and the six members of his squad all glaring back at the camera in full battle rattle in front of an Iraqi palace. Pumpkin had been around 140 pounds of fur and jumbly legs, with a head the size of a basketball. He seemed to smile at Tim from behind the glass. He had been gentle enough to let little kids play on him and even let them pull his lips. But he had snapped into a frenzy of bared canines and snarls when a vagrant came into their backyard in Phoenix. Pumpkin had died when Tim was in college.

I could use a friend like that again, Tim thought as he slid off his desk and out into the heat.

***

Tim drove down one of the countless dirt roads of Uinta County.

"It's like the *Dukes of Hazzard*," he had told a friend on Facebook after he'd first started to explore the unending spiderwebs of lonely roads flanked by irrigation ditches and barbed wire that cut through the cow pastures.

In spite of the dust, the car's windows were all down in an attempt to stay cool as the Dropkick Murphys blared over the noise of the engine.

He was on a mission. The animal shelter, or animal "smelter" as the locals called it because of rumors about animals being euthanized there, was housed on one of the area's many less productive ranches. He pulled into the driveway and drew up before a low clapboard house doing its best to shed its cheap lime-green paint the way people flake off sunburned skin.

A dog might not stop the nightmares, but at least I won't be alone when I wake up screaming.

Tim didn't like to admit that it would also be harder to do something really terrible to himself if it meant leaving someone behind.

He walked up to the front door where a line of deer skulls, antlers still attached, was crudely fastened with baling wire to a gray picket fence. Only after knocking on the door and looking back at the skulls did he realize how nonchalantly he'd just banged on what looked a lot like the door of the house in *The Texas Chainsaw Massacre*.

"Hello," a voice called out from behind him.

Tim started and spun around. Apparently he wasn't completely immune to creepy ranch houses yet. An elderly woman had appeared from around the corner of the building. She wore thick glasses and a faded "Support Our Troops" sweatshirt.

"Hi," Tim said, trying to regain his composure. "I heard that you give dogs to good homes?"

The woman smiled and after they had talked for a while about how hot it was she led him around the back.

"You can have any one of the cats, as long as you tell me which one it is you're taking." She cocked her head at a line of drowsy cats stretched out on hay bales by the big square door of a Quonset hut.

"I keep the dogs inside," she said, pulling the handle on the metal door of the semicircular eyesore of metal as the sound of barking erupted from the near-darkness. She took a leash from a hook on the wall and handed it to Tim. "If you find one, bring it up to the house," she said, before leaving him alone amid the racket and the fetid dog smell.

Tim ventured inside, treading on a roughly poured concrete floor strewn with bits of straw overflowing from the little chainlink cells that separated the occupants. Aussie shepherds and mutt bird dogs yapped at him from their cages. It was like a ranchers' emporium of unwanted cow dogs and hunting hounds, all of dubious pedigrees.

He walked past an unruly boxer-mix and a Blue Tick Heeler with only three legs without pausing, then spotted the curly white hair of a creature almost as big as a baby buffalo in a corner cage ahead. He ignored the other barking creatures and approached the end of the row of cages, where a Great Pyrenees calmly lifted its head and studied him. Its face was like an oversized bowling ball, with squarish features and a giant mouth.

"Hey," Tim whispered, squatting by the animal's cage, careful not to let his knees touch the cement in case dribbles of pee or who-knew-what might be undetected in the dim light.

The dog stood up and approached him, its eyes almost above Tim's own. The creature sniffed the air between itself and Tim and then sat down on its haunches and proffered a massive paw the size of a DVD for him to shake, though he couldn't grip it through the chainlinks.

"I guess you know when you're the big dog in town, huh?" Tim said, smiling as he looked into the brown eyes framed by snow-white fur. Two long rows of teats hung from the dog's abdomen.

"You're a she?" he said, wishing he could stick his hand past the fence and pat the massive head.

The dog came closer and leaned against the cage door, as if reading his impulse. Tim ran his hands over the smooth but dirty fur that protruded through the links, which bowed a little under her weight.

Tim lifted the latch of the gate and snaked the leash in, clipping it to the dog's collar, and then walked her up to the house.

"She's been bred out," the old woman explained. "They used her up to make sheepdog pups and then they dumped her here when she couldn't have no more." The disdain in her voice was obvious. "Got her fixed just to make sure no one tries that again."

"Does she bark at all?" Tim asked.

"Only when the coyotes come," the woman said, with a grin. Apparently this was funny, in a way Tim didn't understand. "No, honey, I don't know—but I've never heard her bark. They do use Pyrenees to guard sheep, though. She might."

"How much?"

"For older dogs we usually want sixty dollars."

Tim nodded. "I'll need to run to the grocery store and get some cash. If I'm back in twenty minutes would that be too late?"

The woman shook her head. "You know where we live. You can just come by and pay us when you have the money. She seems to like you. You can take her now."

"I'll pay you today!" Tim insisted, enchanted but also uncomfortable at how so many people in Meadowlark, like this lady, were so laid back and trusting.

"My granddaughter named her Grover. It's a boy's name, but she was too young to know that she's a she and the dog seems to like it."

Tim thanked her after assuring her again that he would pay her as soon as possible. He folded down the backseats of his Subaru before opening the rear hatch and letting the dog jump in. Grover filled most of the cargo area but seemed to enjoy the ride, panting happily from the open window, her tongue trailing out to flap in the breeze.

Tim couldn't stop staring in the rearview mirror at the giant-headed animal who would now face the world with him.

In the grocery store parking lot he smiled and waved at the strangers who pointed and grinned at the giant dog. Before leaving her in the car to buy some dog food and a new leash, along with sixty dollars in cash, he stopped to stroke her head through the open window and to whisper to her that he would be right back. She wagged her massive tail and panted.

"Tim?"

Tim flinched and spun around, almost bringing his hands up to fight.

Glacial blue eyes. Corn-silk hair...

The nightmare, holding a gallon of milk and a white plastic grocery bag, had caught up with him in the parking lot of Werner's Market.

"Sorry," she said, taken aback by his reaction.

"No, it's okay," he responded, wishing his voice wasn't so shaken and high-pitched. The fact that she still looked like the specter of his nightmare didn't help calm him any.

"Thank you for taking David shooting," she said.

"Yeah." Tim looked down at her grocery bag because he didn't want to look into those eyes. "Did he... *like* it okay?"

"I think so. You know he wants to join the army or The Marines or something?"

Tim nodded.

"It's really good to see him out and doing things. He talks about you a lot."

"I'm afraid I scared him," Tim said before he could stop himself.

"A lot of things seem to scare him." She frowned then beamed at Grover panting beside Tim. "You have a dog!"

"I just got her today."

"She's huge!" Abbey exclaimed, setting her groceries down to reach out for Grover to lick her hand. "I've always wanted a dog, but we've always rented."

"What kind?"

"Like a Newfie or a Tibetan Mastiff. Something big," she said as she ran her hand over the dog's fur.

"We're going to go for a walk in a little bit if you want to come with us," Tim offered. "I also wanted to talk with you a little about David, if that's okay?"

The ice-blue eyes peered a little too deeply into Tim's for comfort before she responded.

CHAPTER 6

On the drive back to the animal shelter Tim kept thinking about how Abbey had finally smiled and said "yes" after leaving him on the hook for a moment. Had she enjoyed that? He sure hadn't. He was supposed to meet her that evening for their walk.

At the house of bleached skulls Tim paid the Support-Our-Troops woman.

"This is for being so punctual," she said, smiling as she handed Tim a jar of what looked like six spherical turds floating in clear liquid.

"They aren't real pretty because they're a little old, but they're some of the best canned peaches you'll ever have."

Tim did his best not to keep the turd jar at arm's length while inspecting them and thanking the old lady.

He felt a little guilty that his excitement over Abbey was overshadowing the new addition to his family as he took Grover into the backyard for a bath with the hose. To his surprise, she patiently put up with the whole ordeal and kept lapping the water flowing from the end. Then he let her hang out in the backyard and eat and drink from her new bowl while he went into the house to clean up.

Just before five he leashed Grover and headed out towards the Jenkins place. What Tim hadn't realized was how far it was from his rental on Maple to Abbey's trailer when he wasn't running. However, taking the dog in the car to Abbey's neighborhood for a walk seemed ridiculous.

"Abbey's just bored," Tim told Grover as they picked up the pace in the evening heat. "I don't think she really wants anything to do with me. She's just taking pity. It's not like there's a lot else to do here."

Tim didn't think he was an attractive guy, but he knew without a doubt that Abbey was beautiful.

The dog seemed to notice Tim's hurried pace and sped up, making sure no slack remained on the thick woven leash. Tim could smell his deodorant doing its job under his clothes and he thanked his luck that he had liberally applied some extra before leaving the house. He had considered putting on some cologne, too, but had thought that might be too much. A little too obvious. Besides, he had never learned how to put the crap on right—always too much or too little.

As the sun was just starting to make the yellow grass on the riverbank turn to amber, he neared the spot where he usually met up with David. His plan was to slow his pace, collect himself and then, radiating confidence and nonchalance, go bang on Abbey's door. It would have worked great, but Abbey stood beside the trail, waiting for him in the same place where David normally did.

"Hey," she said, smiling.

Tim had deliberately dressed casually, but Abbey wore a light pink silky sundress and her short hair had been arranged into complicated swirls and twists that burst from her head like blond firecrackers in the glowing evening light. The ensemble was completed with a pair of black Converse All Star sneakers.

"You look amazing!" Tim heard himself say.

Abbey smiled and joined him as they began their walk along the river. Tim soon found out that Abbey had grown up with her mother and younger half-brother David in Meadowlark, until a scholarship had mercifully delivered her from her mother's trailer and chemical dependency and given her a full ride to the University of Wyoming almost three hundred miles away, where she studied veterinary science.

"Right now, I'm just working with a vet as a tech until David finishes school, then I'll go back."

Tim could feel the heat coming off her bare shoulder as it brushed against his bicep and it made him wonder if she was doing it on purpose.

She's just someone who walks too close, he told himself, *maybe even a little clumsy.*

He wondered the same thing when they came to a wooden bench and she sat down right next to him.

Should I try to hold her hand? Would that ruin everything?

"If you could change anything about the past what would it be?" she asked.

"Wow, you don't play around," Tim said, knowing there was no way he could tell her, even this girl, about the worst moment in his life—though part of him wanted to. "You go first."

"I feel really bad about leaving David."

"What do you mean, you left him?"

"By going away to school, I mean. Mom was using and she was gone most of the time, but then she found another boyfriend who I really didn't trust and I had to get out of there." She frowned and looked down at the All Stars.

"People do what they have to do sometimes," Tim said, though the cliché did little to reassure him about his own past.

"I tell myself that, but…" She shrugged and screwed up her nose.

"I don't think a teenage kid should have to fix everything that you guys were going through. Maybe the blame should rest with the adults." Tim realized this was the first time he had really tried in earnest to connect with anyone since he'd tried to talk to the VA shrink.

"I think I'll feel better if David turns out okay," she said. "Did he," she paused to bite the corner of her lip, "did he tell you he thinks he sees ghosts?"

"Yeah," Tim responded relieved that he wasn't the only one who David had told. "I hope it's okay, but I called the school psychologist to see if maybe he'd talk with David. Would that be all right?"

"Mr. Carson?"

Tim nodded.

"You think he'd do it in the summer?"

"I think he's the kind of guy that just wants to help people, even if school is out. If he can get to his voicemail."

Abbey smiled. "I loved Mr. Carson. He was the one who helped me with the scholarship to UW in the first place."

"He kind of took me under his wing, too," Tim admitted. "He used to nurse an orange juice every day in the breakroom and then pontificate like some cowboy sage."

"That sounds like him," Abbey said, with a smile. "I don't know what his thing is about orange juice, but I always saw him carrying one around on his way to lunch. If he'd talk to David that would be great!" She beamed at Tim, the dipping sun lighting up her hair like flax and turning her skin bronze.

Tim found himself looking down at his own shoes now. It made him nervous to be sitting next to this increasingly enticing creature.

"Have you ever known anyone who said they see ghosts before?"

Tim shook his head. He didn't want to be reminded of his fears about facing the dead woman in the burqa. "I think it might just be how he deals with your mother passing away."

"I hope so, but you have to understand how little either of us really cared about my mom. She was like having another sibling—a bad one, a crazy one, prone to theft and fits—not a parent. This ghost thing seemed to start around the time that David tried to join the football team. He won't tell me all of it—he doesn't want to talk about what happened out there, at the gun place, but since then he seems different."

Tim looked up from his feet. "You think they hurt him or something? Hazed him?"

Abbey picked at one of her nails. "I worried about that. I even looked for cuts or bruises when he walked by in a towel after taking a shower, because he wouldn't talk to me about it. Is that creepy?"

"Not given the circumstances."

"But even before all this, when he was little, sometimes he would talk to people who weren't there and when I'd ask him about it he didn't understand why I couldn't see them."

Tim shrugged. "I had an imaginary friend, too."

"The thing was, when we pulled out a box of family photos for a school project one time, he said that the people in the pictures, some of them anyway, were who he was seeing."

Abbey met Tim's eyes with a solemnity that caught him off guard.

"Do you think some people really can see... you know, that kind of stuff?"

Tim didn't want to answer, but she continued to study him until he relented.

"I do... think something's up," he finally admitted, hoping that doing so wouldn't suddenly bring his wailing nightmare to life in front of him.

"I also worry because my aunt was bona fide nuts and all my relatives are a little crazy, even when they're clean. I just..." She stopped to take a deep breath and when Tim glanced at her he saw the tears starting to form.

"You're doing a good job!" he said, with more feeling than he had felt in a long time. The phrase instantly evoked memories that reached out for him like tendrils of smoke. Something about yelling into the face of another soldier.

Yer doing a good job. The image of a sobbing kid's camo smeared with blood after trying to save his dying buddy. *Yer doing a good job.*

He remembered grabbing a brand new private by his armor and dragging him into a bunker with a splotch of pee on his trousers during a mortar attack. It had become scripture—what Tim told everyone, even when it wasn't true. He had repeated it so often that it had lost much of its meaning, until now.

Sitting next to Abbey, Tim felt himself start to sweat, to dissociate from the present. He worried he would have a freak-out right there. But then her soft hair slid across his chin. He felt her small arms wrap around him and her nose burrow into his chest. And he could hear her crying as his own arms wrapped around her warm little body.

***

The couple walked with Grover back to Abbey's trailer, still holding each other. They watched *30 Days of Night* on her generic flat screen.

"David is playing video games at Merv's house," Abbey explained as she placed a towel down on the green shag carpet for Grover to lie on.

"You ever been to Alaska?" he asked her after they had watched the first ten minutes of the movie about vampires terrorizing Nome, Alaska.

Abbey shook her head. "Have you?"

"I interviewed for a job in Fairbanks."

"Was it really like this?" she asked, cocking her chin at the screen.

"Overrun with vampires? Yeah they were all over the place. In fact," he continued, pointing at the lead bloodsucker on the screen, "that was the one who interviewed me. He said that most young vampires really just don't have the appreciation for *Catcher in the Rye* and *Animal Farm* that they should."

"I would think they'd be more into *Dracula*," Abbey grinned. "I mean, is it dark all the time in the winter?"

"That's what they say. Mostly I wanted to move up there because it's cold."

"Why do you want it to be cold?"

Tim wanted to blow it off, to avoid telling the full truth. To simply tell her, *I hate the heat*, but instead he heard himself say, "You know what PTSD is?"

Abbey nodded.

"I don't know if that's what it really is," he went on, pausing to watch one of the vampires on screen rip someone's throat open. "It seems pretty trite, too brief an acronym for what it's really like, but whenever I feel hot like I did in Iraq, or something happens here that reminds me of something back there, I kind of..." He dreaded using the word. So overdramatic, so Hollywood, but with Abbey's sympathetic eyes on him he steeled himself to say it. "I kind of... *flashback* to things that happened. I find myself forced to relive something that occurred there."

He didn't want to look directly at Abbey, but finally did.

"This summer must be horrible, huh?" she replied, wrapping both of her hands around his.

"These have been the worst few weeks of my life since coming home," Tim admitted, realizing after saying it that in fact they had been. "I worry..." He hesitated, her eyes were on him. "I worry a lot about flipping out. I wouldn't hurt anyone or whatever, but I just don't want people to think I'm crazy."

She nodded understandingly. "I've seen a few flip-outs, Tim. You don't grow up where I did and not have some crazy things happen."

"Abbey," he added surprised that he seemed able to talk like this to a person he'd only known for about sixteen hours, "I also feel like I'm not... *worthy* of anything good."

"What do you mean?"

"I feel guilty."

"About what?"

"I killed someone."

Abbey nodded slowly. Her face the most empathetic thing Tim had ever seen and for the first time in as long as he could remember he felt safe with someone.

"I thought that's what people did over there," she said.

Tim shook his head. "I shot a mother in the face while she held her dead baby."

Abbey's expression dropped.

CHAPTER 7

Tim lay in bed, trying to sleep. Since moving to Wyoming he had started to borrow Louis L'Amour novels from the library and read them as he lay in bed. They were horrible, and perfect to fall asleep to, but tonight his copy of *Bendigo Shafter* lay spread on the carpet with its spine up.

Sweating in the heat under an oscillating fan that did little but stir up the hot air, he couldn't believe he had told Abbey about the Iraqi woman. He had only told one other person about that, so why had he picked someone he had just met? What kind of girl wants to be around someone after you've told her that you killed a mother holding her dead child?

Tim glanced at his Blackberry. 2:17 a.m.

He rolled onto his side and texted, *Abbey R U awake?* He let the sweaty phone slip out of his hand and onto the dresser. To his surprise, the phone chimed a moment later.

Yes u ok?

He picked the phone up and called her.

"Hey, I don't know if you want to talk, but… I'm really sorry that I told you that."

"I'm not."

"No, it wasn't fair," he said. "I don't think I deserve to be around people, good people like you, after what I did. Sometimes I try to chase people off."

"It didn't work. Besides, I don't know if I'm good people."

"You are."

The line went quiet for a while.

"You pushing people away hasn't brought anyone back, has it?"

Tim frowned. "I guess not. I just think you deserve to be around someone who *hasn't* done what I did and I don't think I deserve to be around someone like you."

"Are you trying to dump me?" she said, laughing.

"Dump you? No. I... I'm just saying I'm a hard person to live with because of what I did."

"Tim, have you ever tried hanging out with any of the guys here? You have all your teeth and you've never given your cousin a six-pack of Mountain Dew so you can feel her up in a Walmart bathroom! You're a keeper."

"That happened to you?"

"No," she snickered, "but I don't think that's fiction for some people here. Seriously, *you* are doing a good job, Tim," she said, copying what he had said earlier. "Maybe you need to give yourself a break."

He didn't know what to say.

"Can I come to your house tomorrow?" she asked.

"Yeah. Why?"

"Sometimes I just want to get out of this place."

"I'll make something," Tim offered.

"You can cook?"

"Well, I know how to cook one thing, anyway."

"One thing sounds great! Try to get some sleep, okay? Night."

She hung up.

Tim lay back and sweated on the bed, thinking of the way the sun had turned Abbey's hair to gold.

You're doing a good job, Tim.

He slept for one hour and twelve minutes before he heard the soft footsteps of someone moving down the hall towards his closed bedroom door.

Pretend to sleep.

The movement stopped just as a shadow appeared in the

crack under the door. Grover leapt to her feet and charged the door, growling and baring a row of teeth. Tim jerked open the dresser drawer, scooped the pistol's bulbous rubber grip into his right hand and rolled off the side of the bed away from the door. Squatting behind the mattress and box springs he pointed the gun at the door.

"Who's there?" he shouted.

The shadow at the crack under the door remained.

Tim cocked the gun and yelled again. "Get out!"

The shadow did not leave. Instead, it walked right through the closed door. Blue eyes framed by white-blonde hair, bloated green skin, a cut on the right side of her lips… it walked right through the hollow core door like it wasn't even there.

Grover barked and jumped angrily while retreating a good six feet back. Tim pointed the weapon at the apparition's chest and attempted to align the shaking sights over its sternum, though he wanted to drop the gun and run.

The woman still wore the same billowy, rough-knitted red sweater with a green Christmas tree on it. Her hands moved from her sides to her abdomen. Something was wrapped around her right wrist. It looked like a chocolate-brown extension cord. Her knuckles were cut and oozing thick rust-colored blood. He expected the girl to produce that unholy, disgusting, dead child from somewhere beneath her clothes, but instead she ran her hands around her belly, the way a pregnant woman might, and then Tim noticed the bulge under the billowy sweater, the beginnings of life poking through her gaunt frame.

Her alabaster countenance focused on him as her cracked lips mouthed the words, *"Help me!"*

Tim couldn't look away. Feeling like a mouse in the eyes of a cobra, he nodded at the figure as if in agreement to her request. Then she turned and walked back through the bedroom door, leaving a silhouette of ice on the wood.

His breath plumed into ice crystals in the freezing room, blowing out like smoke over the front sight of his gun. He became aware of a sick churning in his stomach that threatened to make him soil himself like the several times he almost had in Iraq.

Tim didn't want to believe it had been real, but the silhouette of ice remained on the door—head and shoulders, about five and a half feet tall.

He stepped back and slid down the wall, feeling the wall's frosty touch on his bare skin. For a long time he sat on the floor, his weapon pointed at the white ice shadow on the door until it slowly dissolved away to nothing.

CHAPTER 8

Someone was banging on the front door. Tim's eyes, still facing the bedroom door, snapped open. The morning heat was suffocating.

The pounding did not stop.

"I'm coming!"

The pistol gleamed in the early sun from the carpet, where it must have dropped when he fell asleep as he waited for the nightmare to return.

He checked the bedroom door for any trace of ice. Nothing. He picked up the gun and put it in the nightstand drawer.

In spite of the banging out front, he paused to inspect the door once more, extending his fingertips to gingerly run them in an arc over where the apparition had appeared. The wood felt warm as everything else in the house and Tim felt relieved. He glanced back at the dresser drawer, which now contained the gun. Had he pulled the pistol in his sleep? He stood to one side of the door and flung it open, then carefully peeked around the door frame, half expecting to see his grisly visitor hanging out in the long hallway that led to the living room. Grover shot out the open bedroom door towards the front door, where the knocking continued.

There was no one in the house, just the morning rays of sun hitting the old shag carpet and the incessant pounding on the door. Tim's eyes passed over the spot where the apparition had stood. He remembered the cold prickle of ice on his bare skin almost as if something had reached out from the previous night's encounter and poked him with a dirty fingernail to say, "That wasn't a dream. I'm still here!"

"I'm coming!" Tim shouted a second time. He hurried down the hall, eager not to be in the bedroom any longer. When he reached the main entry he peeked past the curtain by the door to see David standing on his porch in full running gear.

For the first time Tim felt genuinely delighted to see the boy. He really wanted to get out of the house and felt relieved that he hadn't scared David off with his antics at the range. He opened the door and snaked his head around it, keeping his boxer-clad frame out of sight.

"Hey, Dave, you ready?" he asked.

"It's nine a.m.," the boy pointed out.

"I just got to put something on," he said, as Grover tried to squeeze out the crack of the partially opened door. "See if she has to pee," he said, opening the door wider to let the dog out.

Tim hastened back to his room and grabbed a pair of shorts and a t-shirt, which he put on in the living room. Then he grabbed his running shoes from their spot by the back door and went out front to sit on the porch as he laced them up.

"How 'bout that burger afterwards?" Tim asked, wanting an excuse not to go back home straight after the run.

They put the reluctant dog back inside, knowing that she wouldn't keep up with them, and set off for the jogging trail.

"What did you do last night?" Tim asked, hoping to distract himself.

"Played Zombie Nazis with Jim and Merv."

Tim nodded, trying to shake off the distraction of what had happened last night. Part of him wanted to tell someone about it, but he had given David enough trouble already. He couldn't imagine saying, "By the way twice now I've seen someone who looks a lot like your sister acting like the living dead—what do you think is up with that?"

They're just bad dreams, stress-induced nightmares, flash-

backs, whatever.

The duo passed David's home. Tim looked over his shoulder as they ran by, hoping to catch a glimpse of Abbey.

"My sister's at work," David said.

Tim felt slightly embarrassed that he had been caught. For such a spacey, weird kid it was funny what Dave noticed and what he didn't.

"Did she say anything about me?" Tim asked hesitantly.

"She said she's going to eat with you tonight."

Tim hadn't thought to ask David if he wanted to come.

"You like pizza?" Tim asked. "You're not one of these guys who can't eat gluten, or cheese, or whatever—right?"

"I'm good."

"Remind me when we get a burger to give you a twenty for pizza. I'll lend you whatever DVDs I have, and you can borrow any of my Xbox games, too."

"Can we go shooting again some time?" the boy asked.

Tim turned in surprise. "Sure."

"I'm going to start a paper route next week and I can pay for the bullets if you tell me what kind to get."

"Don't worry about the ammo. I'll buy it."

"You sure?"

"Yeah. You've been helping me stay in shape. I should pay you. We can even go shoot somewhere else if you'd," Tim broke off as he searched for some other phrase than "feel more comfortable. If you want."

"The range is okay."

Tim glanced at David to see if he was playing tough. As usual, the kid couldn't be read very well.

They finished their miles and, instead of getting cleaned up, ran straight to the burger place for an early lunch. To Tim's surprise David ordered a complete meal and forwent the corn dog for a double cheeseburger.

"You trying to break me?" said Tim, smiling.

"I want to put on more weight, develop more muscle mass," David answered.

For the first time since Tim had met the awkward gangly boy the duo actually started to have a decent two-sided conversation. Mostly it was about military stuff, about what David would need to do to survive basic training. Tim urged him to make sure he went to college and ROTC or Officers' Candidate School.

The boy picked his teeth with his soda straw for a moment.

"Do you think I'm stable?" he asked at last. "You know—enough for the military, anyway. The recruiter on the phone asked a bunch of questions about if I'd ever been arrested, or smoked pot, or if I'd ever seen a psychologist."

I dunno, Tim thought. "Yeah… they ask those kinds of questions. I think you're fine, Dave."

"Even if… I've seen things?"

"Yep!" Tim certainly didn't feel qualified anymore to judge who was crazy or not. "In fact, I'd like for you to talk with Mr. Carson sometime soon, if that's cool."

"I'm worried that if I do I can't join."

Tim shook his head. "Having talked to someone in psych doesn't disqualify you from military service if you do want to do it. Most guys who don't talk to one before they leave end up talking to them on their way back." He hesitated, realizing what he was about to say. "If you want to talk to a shrink or… me," he added awkwardly, "about whatever it is that bugs you it'll be okay. Even if you tell the recruiter that you talked to Mr. Carson all he'll do is tell you not to tell anyone else."

David looked thoughtful for a long time before he said anything.

"Yesterday, when we went to the gun range, I really did see what I told you." The cup in the boy's hands trembled slightly. "Her eyes and the color of her hair were exactly the same as my sister's."

"Why do you think you saw her?"

David frowned. "I don't know why I see them. I guess I always have. It just wasn't until the football team thing that I saw one that looked like Abbey."

Tim looked out the window and wondered what had happened to the fat chocolate lab who had visited Chuck's the other day. He knew what he had to ask next, but didn't want to.

"Did she have something wrapped around her wrist?"

The boy shrugged. "I couldn't see."

Tim nodded slowly. The boy sounded like the psychics on TV who suddenly go vague under a line of unexpected questioning.

"She wore a sweater, though. An ugly one, the kind we had at the ugly sweater Christmas party at school."

***

This is why you don't get close to people!

Tim opened the cupboard door above the stove and found the familiar brown cardboard box hiding behind the pepper and garlic powder. He stared at it for a while, having not touched it since he'd moved into the house almost a year before.

I don't know where else I'm going to find the ingredients in this town.

He drummed his fingers on the counter. Reluctantly, he slid the more commonly used fixings aside that he'd already laid out and pulled down the box. The little brown parcel had traveled almost all the way around the world and back again, from a desert in Phoenix to another one in Iraq. Tim had collected it with a shipment of DVDs as "Let The Bodies Hit The Floor" hammered through a pair of tinny speakers at mail call. While other guys flicked out their Gerbers and slit open logs of Copenhagen or back issues of *Maxim*, Tim had cut the packing tape on the box from his mother and taken it back behind his platoon's tent, where Specialist Gilmore was reading *Born on a Blue Day* on a lawn chair.

"Check it out," Tim said, setting the box down next to him on the beat-up metal bookshelf of paperbacks that passed for their company's library. Inside were two packets of rice noodles and yellow curry, flanked by cans of coconut milk and tuna fish.

"Nice!" Gilmore said, putting his book down to inspect the new supplies with the eagerness of a kid on Christmas morning.

Gilmore was the only guy who would be that excited about getting a box of ingredients. Anything falling short of verboten pornography or Jack Daniels would not garner so much interest in anyone else Tim knew in Iraq.

Still wearing their body armor, and still keeping their rifles at arm's reach, the two "college boy" enlistees boiled the rice noodles, using several MRE heaters, and mixed in curry and coconut milk in the oversized metal mugs they'd been issued, amid the smoke of other people's cigarettes.

While other guys who'd gotten lucky at mail wolfed down beef jerky and Oreos sent to them by moms, or VFWs, or schoolkids, Gilmore and Tim ate the closest thing they'd had to Thai food in months. They stretched out on lawn chairs and cardboard supply cases, almost believing the lie that they were on the biggest beach in the world. Two kids still clinging to the idea that they were only there to help rebuild, as carpenters and masons in the Army Corps of Engineers.

Back in his kitchen, Tim pulled a paring knife from the rack and slit open the clear packing tape of the re-sealed box, then popped the flaps. He took a long slow breath of the curried smell of that day and remembered the last time he'd seen Gils happy.

"I'm sorry about what happened, Gils," Tim said to the open box on his kitchen counter in Meadowlark. "I did everything I could, but it didn't make any difference."

Tim caught a mental flash of Gilmore jerking back after an incoming round made his throat explode with a burst of blood that sprayed like a popped cyst, coating the squad with blood and a tarnished copper smell they would remember forever. They'd told Tim in the Combat Lifesaver course that people have about one and a half gallons of blood in their bodies, but when it is leaking out over sweat-soaked body armor, staining name tapes and turning sticky black in one hundred and twenty degrees of heat, it seemed like so much more. He remembered feeling the tube-like jugular under his friend's skin—no latex, no protection, just fingers clotting in the dying kid's life fluid—as the helo finally landed and his friends, frightened and confused, attempted a ring of three hundred and sixty degree security around the bird, pointing rifles they had never fired in anger, as Vasquez and Wilson helped Tim drag Gilmore to the steel angel.

As the chopper lurched off the ground Tim felt Gilmore go very still and he wanted the gunner to slaughter the guilty ones who had turned his best friend into a greying ghost before they ever made it to the surgical unit. Once they landed he waited outside, shocked and numb, for the news he knew was coming.

"I hope this is cool, man," Tim said to the box. "I haven't had Thai food since that day, but I don't know where I'm going to buy this stuff in Meadowlark and I don't normally make any-thing more fancy than sandwiches. If you saw her, if you met her, maybe you'd understand." He sighed. "If it had happened to me, if I'd died back there, maybe after a while I'd want you to use the curry and eat the noodles with a girl you really liked, too." He could feel the tears coming. "I wish I'd told you that I was glad to have someone over there who I could be me around."

As he ran his hand over his eyes and looked down at the wet-ness on the edge of his palm Tim wondered vaguely when the last time had been that he'd cried. He let out a long breath then removed the ingredients, lining them up along the counter like they were forming for an inspection.

Tim pulled two chicken breasts from the fridge, diced them, then slid the meat off his cutting board into a pan that he placed on the stove. He turned on the burner and began to add the sandy yellow curry to the chicken, along with basil and chopped cloves of garlic.

Looking for a pot under the counter, he wondered what to do with Gil's empty box. He thought about using it to store ammunition or maybe some of his remaining tactical gear. He set the pot down and picked up the box, then walked down the hall to his closed bedroom door. "If you're here, Gils, I need you to have my back," he whispered in the dark silence of the hall.

Tim reached tentative fingers towards the doorknob and remembered how it felt to have Gilmore behind him in the stack when they were ordered to put aside their masonry squares and accompany a series of raids. He remembered the very smell of Gils as they had waited dry-mouthed and queasy in other silent hallways for the kick or thundering bang that opened other doors and they surged into people's homes and lives, kicking things out of their way and barking orders in bad Arabic, running on pure adrenaline and terror. They had been like apocalyptic trick-or-treaters or incarnations of *A Clockwork Orange's* droogs.

Tim would have given anything for Gils to be the angel on his shoulder as he reached for his own doorknob there in the Wyoming rental. A quick twist and then Tim rushed his door and plowed into the bedroom where he had seen the ghost.

Empty. Unbearably hot.

He let out a slow breath, thankful not to feel a chill, then turned back to the door relieved not to find a skiff of ice on it either. He crossed to the closet and pulled Gil's copies of *Born on a Blue Day*, *Confessions of a Sociopath*, and *The Mummy at The Dining Room Table: Eminent Therapists Reveal Their Most Unusual Cases and What They Teach Us About Human Behavior* from the top shelf and placed them in the box. They were the last of the books Gils had carried around as part of his informal studies to become a psychologist after the war. Tim placed the box in the bottom of the closet, keeping one eye on the open bedroom door, and then retreated to the kitchen, closing the door behind him.

Grabbing the pot, he began to fill it in the sink. He was annoyed with himself that he hadn't done that first, so that it could have started boiling.

They had used to think they could fight anything. At least, that was the lie the two "smart" guys had passed between them after they had some experience firing back at the muzzle flares and moving figures that started shooting at them. They had always surrendered to the impulse to aim a little high, reducing the risk of actually hitting anyone—until, that is, Gilmore was ripped away, bloody and dying.

Tim ground black pepper over his chicken curry as it began

to sizzle in the heat of the Teflon-coated pan. Then it occurred to him. *Crap!* He shot across the kitchen and seized his cell phone.

"Hey, Abbey," he said after she picked up. "Are you a vegetarian?"

"No," she said.

"So chicken's all right?"

"That'd be great," she said. "You okay?" She sounded a little worried.

"Oh, yeah, I just forgot to ask."

"Thanks. I'll be over at six."

Tim hung up and stirred the chicken with an old wooden spoon. His mother had given it to him when he moved out of the dorms his sophomore year.

He started thinking about Gils again. Having shut out any thought of an afterlife for fear of one day confronting the woman with the dead child, he wondered what it would be like to have Gils watching over him, if that were possible.

If I'm going to Hell, will Gils be there?

It seemed unlikely that good old Gils would be there. After all, he hadn't done what Tim had. He'd died innocent and clean, before all the awful stuff really started.

The chicken had turned the rubbery tan color of cooked poultry. He added freshly cut broccoli and coconut milk, lemon juice, fish oil and, of course, more yellow curry. He tasted the sauce and felt it bite his tongue and warm his throat with the flavor of salt and sweet coconut milk. Nodding his head in appreciation, like a hillbilly sampling moonshine, he drained the noodles and added his sauce.

***

Abbey arrived right at six, wearing a "hello kitty" t-shirt with jeans and sandals.

Tim stared at her in the doorway with a dumbstruck expression, not sure what to say. She leaned over the threshold and Tim felt like a lotto winner when she embraced him. He led her into the kitchen and instantly hated himself when she saw the table set with candles.

It's so corny! Overplayed, stupid. She's wearing a t-shirt. You've misread her!

"This is amazing!" she said.

"It's not too much?"

"What do you mean?" she asked, approaching the pot on the stove. "That smells wonderful. I was eighteen before I ever had Thai food."

"You're kidding!" Tim said, grabbing a pair of pot holders and carrying the curry over to the table.

Abbey shook her head and pulled open a drawer by the stove. "You keep your silverware right where my Grandma used to."

"What?"

"This used to be my grandmother's house. She kept her forks and spoons in the same drawer."

"Why didn't you tell me?"

"I just got here," she said as she extracted knives and forks from the drawer to set the table.

"Was David ever here?"

"Yeah, but I don't think he'd remember it," she said as she placed the cutlery on either side of the plates Tim had placed. "This house is still one of the best things I remember about being a little girl."

"How often were you here?" Tim asked as they sat down to eat.

"I think from part of first grade off and on through third," she answered. "Sometimes my mom would drop me off here at weekends and when I got older I'd call Grandma when things were too crazy at our house and she'd come pick me up and then David, too."

"She treated you all right, then?"

"Oh, Grandma was great. It was my mom who kept wanting to take us back." Abbey frowned as she twisted her fork into the noodles.

"Grandma always made sure that I ate something. She took me up to the Uintas sometimes to fish. I remember she had a huge tub of garage-sale Legos in the front room and at night we'd watch PBS specials about animals and Africa—stuff like that. There wasn't a cable company here then and PBS was the only thing you could get clearly on rabbit ears. I loved this place."

"So, basically, you're using me to feel closer to your grandma?" Tim asked in a tone of mock disappointment.

"Basically, yeah," Abbey said, nodding. "In fact, I'm going to need you to work on some homemade cookies while I see if Mr. Rogers is on." She smiled at him above her plate of half-eaten noodles.

After they finished eating Tim cleared Abbey's plate for her and sat it down next to Grover so she could lick it clean. He worried that it might gross Abbey out, but she simply leaned over and petted the dog while Grover pre-soaked the dishes.

"Where was your grandpa?" he asked as he sat the glasses in the sink.

"I never knew him. He died before I was born." She helped him package the leftovers into a Tupperware container and then put them in the fridge.

"Tim!"

He spun around in alarm as she pulled the jar of turd-peaches from the fridge.

We've had a near-perfect time and now she's going to think I'm some sort of pseudo Howard Hughes weirdo who keeps his feces in jars in the fridge!

"The lady who sold me Grover gave me those. I'll throw them away," he said hastily, reaching for the jar.

"Why would you throw them away?"

"'Cause they look like crap in a jar! I'd been saving them so I could figure out how peaches could ever look like that."

"You can't throw these away!" Abbey insisted on placing the jar on the counter and twisting the lid. "They taste better the longer they've aged like this."

Tim cringed as she grabbed a fork and fished one from the jar and bit into one of the brown masses.

"Try it!" she said, holding out the half-eaten brown peach on a fork.

"Uh..."

"C'mon!"

He leaned in and bit a chunk of the peach off, trying to think about how Abbey's mouth had just kissed it.

Pure sugar.

"Wow!"

"You're one of us now," she said, smirking. "A fellow yokel, eating peach preserves from a jar that's probably old enough to have had moonshine in it at one time."

Still holding the peaches, she walked to the living room and began to explore Tim's massive collection of DVDs, placed on their shelves like fine china.

"I got really bored in Iraq," Tim explained. "I started buying them on Amazon and people started mailing them to me, too. We even used them like money sometimes, like cigarettes in prison."

"I just picture a lot of guys watching a lot of porn," she said.

"Uh... I didn't do anything like that. I still haven't seen anyone naked, not even me." Tim said, doing his best Bill Murray deadpan.

She laughed. "Can we watch one?"

"A porn?"

"No!" She pointed at the shelves of DVDs.

"I'd love that."

"When I was little I quit watching TV for a while. I remember seeing how everyone's life seemed perfect and I felt mad and jealous because I realized ours wasn't like that."

She thumbed through the DVDs. "One of my mom's boyfriends had a fit when I'd watch *The Fresh Prince of Bel-Air*, because they were black. I didn't understand what the big deal was. They were nice and their house was clean. It was more than I could say for us. It wasn't until I went to college that I realized everyone, even people whose lives *are* almost perfect, think that there's something wrong with them. They think there's some perfect place or whatever."

"I know what you mean."

"I loved this show," she said, holding up the second season of the *X-Files*.

They watched the first fifteen minutes of the first episode on the couch until their interest in the now dated, cheesy, show waned and they started to hold hands, then to cuddle, and then finally to make out.

Tim gave Abbey a ride home around two in the morning.

"I don't want to weird David out," she explained.

She gave Tim a quick peck on the porch and he insisted that she lock all her doors and windows before she went to sleep, which earned a funny look in response.

"I just want you to be safe," he said. He almost felt comfortable enough with her to say, *Well, you see, I've been having these premonitions that something horrible will happen to you and…* But he didn't.

She smiled and kissed him again and Tim went home, where he slept incredibly well in his spare bedroom. He was in no hurry to go back into his own room, despite his having cleared it with the memory of Gilmore at his back.

CHAPTER 9

At seven in the morning Tim woke up once again to the sound of someone banging on his front door. Grover leapt up and ran to the living room.

"Just a minute, Dave!" Tim hollered groggily.

He stumbled towards his room for his running clothes, wishing the horrible thud would quit ringing as the vibrations of it were starting to invade his skull.

"I'm coming!" he hollered, peering into his bedroom at the threshold before scurrying inside and pulling his running clothes from his dresser. He went out into the hall and dressed, still giving weary glances into his room.

Finally, he went to the living room and opened the door.

Lieutenant Yates, the barrel-chested cop who had interviewed Tim and all of Heather Brady's other teachers during his fruitless investigation into her murder, stood on his porch.

"Hello," Tim said, a little confused as to why this fireplug of a man blocked his doorway.

Grover shot through the opened door and made for the lawn.

"Mr. Ross, Tim, I need your help. There's a girl missing from the girls' camp up in the Uinta Range. They say you did something with helicopters in the army? Aviation?"

"Who said that?" Tim shook his head, wondering what piece of small-town gossip the man had picked up as he tried not to think of that one time he'd been lifted into the air holding Gilmore. "I've only been in a helicopter once."

The trooper frowned. "Well, we need all the help we can get, and that's one time more than anyone else here. You think you can help someone try to spot things from the air?"

Tim didn't want to go in a helicopter again. "I'll do what I can. Is it a kid I'd know?" he asked as he let the dog back into the house.

"I'll brief you on the way," Yates said as he turned towards the cruiser parked in the driveway.

Tim followed Yates to his car and pulled open the passenger door. He eyed the computer screen on the console and the shotgun sprouting from between the seats. He slid in and smelled stale coffee.

"Yesterday evening, Cassidy Heintz disappeared after she left the archery range at the girls' camp," the cop explained as they pulled into the street and headed towards the main part of town. "The adults and the kids started looking for her and then we got the call late last night."

"They know why she left?" Tim asked.

The trooper shook his head. "She was supposed to help make dinner at the mess. When her group showed up to eat and they saw she wasn't there they started looking."

"You think it has anything to do with Heather Brady?"

"I hope not," the cop said in a surprisingly earnest tone. "She's my niece."

"I'm sorry."

"Don't be sorry. Let's just find her."

"Does she go to Meadowlark?"

"Fillmore," he said, naming the only other high school in the county, Meadowlark High's rival. "She's the captain of the volleyball team. Got almost straight As. Her idiot father ran out on her just after Christmas, but she's hanging in there."

"Where's Dad?"

"I called and confirmed he's been in Texas all month. He's supposed to get here tonight to help look."

Yates took his right hand off the wheel and dug in his back

pocket. The car weaved a little.

"I don't have any more photocopies with me but," he extract-ed his wallet and flipped through it clumsily with one hand, "that's her." He handed the open wallet to Tim.

A teenage girl in a volleyball uniform grinned back at him. Blonde, but not especially pretty. Tim looked at her face the way you always did when you heard of someone missing, as if their picture could tell you what had happened.

"That was taken last fall, but more or less it's her." Yates took the wallet back from Tim and looked up at the saw-toothed sprawl of the Uinta Mountains along the southern horizon. "We've lost more people in those mountains in the last twenty years than really ought to have gone missing." His face looked haunted as he watched the jagged peaks roll past the passenger window.

"Like, hunting accidents?" Tim asked, remembering how excited the kids in his class were when deer season started and phones were passed around displaying pictures of deer and elk they had bagged.

"I've never seen a set of ridges swallow up so many normal, sane people who were just going fishing or camping right by their trucks at the lake. They just... disappear."

Tim's attention focused on the baseball diamond at the mu-nicipal park where a small bubble of a helicopter did its best to suck up and spit away the grass of the infield. A group of people at one of the picnic shelters across the parking lot hand-ed out photocopies with the girl's picture. Men wearing hunter orange vests, some with dogs, stood at the back of a pickup listening to Yates' underling, Officer Farner, give orders and gesticulate. Yates brought the cruiser to a lurching stop at the curb in the parking lot and led the way towards the chopper, stopping a respectful distance from the spinning blades.

"The guy inside is Mike Dennis," he shouted at Tim. "This is as far as I go." The trooper gestured at him to get aboard. "Thank you, Mr. Ross," he added, proffering his hand.

Tim wished he could have said something comforting, but instead he just shook the man's hand before shooting towards the chopper by the pitcher's mound.

Squinting through the whirling dust, Tim steeled himself against the encroaching memory brought on by the noise and smell of the exhaust. It hit him with a familiarity that took him straight back to the day when he and Vasquez and Wilson had ducked low as they carried Gilmore away in a poncho.

He reached up and covered his nose to shut out the exhaust smell.

It's okay, it's all right. Keep it together. You're here, not there.

He ran with his hand outstretched to find the latch on the door.

Just a few more yards!

Tim worried about being pushed back to that awful place, sucked into a vortex of swirling grit and the memory of Gilmore looking up with dead fish eyes into the helicopter's rotors as they loaded him into the chopper. Then his outstretched palm found the hot steel of the door latch. He pulled the hatch open and slid inside, slamming the door shut behind him and twisting its latch closed without even looking at the pilot.

A photocopy of Cassidy's yearbook photo taped beside the console of the chopper stared back at Tim. The pilot handed him a headset and he put it on.

"I'm Mike," the man said, his voice coming in clipped and crisp through the headset. "You been in one of these before?"

Tim nodded and gave him a thumbs-up.

"Any questions?"

Tim shook his head.

"Okay, we'll see what we can do."

Without another word, the pilot took the spinning beast straight up into the air. The jolt of a vertical take-off was just as Tim remembered it, a stomach-wrenching movement that shook his bowels and made an already nervous stomach even more jumpy. The chopper roared over the park as it climbed past the rooftops of the small Wyoming town. Staring out the window, Tim hoped to remind himself that the green grass of the baseball field, the picnic shelter of the park and all the neat little houses below were a classic American mosaic and that he was still here and not back there.

The pilot veered left at the river and then started towards the mountains, which were still capped with snow despite the heat of late summer. Tim looked carefully for Abbey's house, hoping he might see her in the yard, but no one was out front, and her tiny Tercel was gone. The unrelenting heat had turned the pastures that surrounded the outskirts of town brown.

They passed over the church camp where the disappearance had been reported, making low circles that spiraled larger and larger with each pass. Tim could see the occasional building or green canvas tent poking through the tree cover. He could even make out people dressed in hunter orange milling around as they looked for Cassidy.

"That's the cabin where they found that one girl," Mike said, pointing to a tiny, forlorn collection of rough-hewn logs and a roof made of more holes than shingles in a sagebrush-covered clearing. "Tragedy," he added, shaking his head.

The site looked just like the pictures in the *Meadowlark Call* printed beneath the headline, "Brady Found Slain."

Unlike the professionally taken picture of Cassidy Heintz taped to the instrument panel, all Heather Brady had ever received was a picture of the eerie cabin where the police said she had been strangled. The paper never printed a good one of her alive. In fact, the only one Tim had ever seen looked like it had been taken on a webcam. Copies of it had been fastened to light poles and post office bulletin boards under the word "Missing" long after Heather quit showing up to Tim's English class.

Brady had spent most of her time in the second row, third seat back of Tim's English class working on her make-up or playing with her phone. When she did talk to anyone it usually consisted of bragging about how much better Beverly Hills was than Meadowlark, Wyoming. This had annoyed the crap out of Tim. When one of his students asked the question, "If you lived in Beverly Hills, why are you here? This isn't Jackson!" Tim heard himself laughing with the rest of the class before he could stop himself. Rich Californians and New Yorkers had a fetish for "Western Life," but only as long as they were permitted to indulge their fantasies in opulent places like Jackson or Cody, with ski slopes and twelve-dollar coffees and lots of "cute little shops." Not places that lived off of mining and ranching like Meadowlark.

The third week of her late start, Heather had bragged about a boyfriend no one had ever heard of in the small town. She would occasionally bring in a new purse or a new article of black clothing that covered too little for the fall weather. She told people that "Jake" had bought it for her.

"Where's Jake go to school?" one of the students asked her.

"He doesn't go to school. He's older."

"What's his last name?" one of the other kids asked.

"I can't tell you," she told them, in a loaded tone.

"Why not?" the kid sneered. "Because he's not real?"

During Yates's brief interviews with Heather's teachers, Tim had mentioned Jake and had been told "we'll look into it." Tim had never heard anything more about it and had assumed like his students that Jake was an imaginary boyfriend.

In late November Heather had quit coming to school and most people were grateful not to have to listen to it anymore. Unlike Cassidy Heintz, a popular kid with a cop for an uncle, no one had seemed to raise a fuss over Heather. Even her mother, a waitress at the Flying J Truck Stop thought she had run away for weeks before the missing posters appeared.

Tim and the pilot were passing back over the camp again, hoping the red camp-issued t-shirt Cassidy was last seen in might poke through the trees. However, the only people they saw were other searchers.

The bird finally turned and landed again at the baseball diamond, where even more people were checking in at the park, filling up on water and Gatorade from big orange coolers and eating sandwiches donated by the grocery store deli.

Tim waited for the rotors to quit spinning before getting out of the craft, hoping not to be reminded again of memories of Gilmore and Iraq. Then he stepped out carefully and breathed through his mouth until he'd moved well clear of the machine.

***

It was cool up in the Uinta Range as Tim and the other searchers did their best to keep each other in sight. The overhanging branches of the trees cast cobweb-like shadows over his face as he walked through a forest weirdly dark and chilly in spite of how hot it had been in town.

Each group had a leader with a GPS and each searcher carried a yellow whistle and a now well-Xeroxed photo of the girl in her volleyball uniform. They marched side by side up and down the now gridded-out mountain. Tim's team roved about

half a mile from the camp, headed up slope because the searches down slope found nothing. So far Cassidy Heintz remained
a ghost. There was no radio crackle coming in to the group
leader of clothing, or footprints or blood or any other sign of
a one hundred and twenty pound teenager who had suddenly
been swallowed up into the black-limbed forest.

They did their best to keep each other in sight. Their safety
orange shirts and vests, normally reserved for the hunting
season or for road crew gigs, would occasionally flash or pop
up through the brush as individual searchers reassured each
other that they were not alone.

"Over here!"

Tim spun to see Merv Vietti, one of his fourth period students waving to the other searchers. He braced himself against
the thought of what they might see as the orange figures con-
verged on the kid and stared down at something in the fallen
pine needles.

Approaching the teen, whose look of confusion was turning
to fear, Tim followed his gaze and spotted several small white
clumps lying amid the dead pine needles, something like little
mushrooms or pebbles.

Merv took a knee and poked at one with an outstretched
finger. Then Tim saw the familiar four points of the roots and
the bumpy contours of the crowns.

They were teeth. Yellow-white bicuspids.

"Are those her teeth?" someone asked.

The assembled men frowned at each other.

"They're teeth all right," Carl Pender said gravely, poking
at them with his search stick. "I bet the rest are nearby." He
turned and eyed the grass at the edge of the clearing.

Tim felt a growing sense of familiar dread wash over him
as Pender, a professional outfitter and guide, walked towards

the brush. Tim's mind flashed back to that place of heat and gunfire, where a sickly-sweet stench and the buzzing of insects would pull them toward a growing smell until they would come upon a corpse. Sometimes it would have a grey-green cast to the bloated skin on its swollen face. Sometimes there would be no face or head at all. Sometimes the eyes were gouged out and Tim wasn't sure if that was better or worse than when the eyes remained, wide and terrified—a testament to the last horrifying moment they would ever know.

Pender fixed on something in the grass and carefully ran the tip of his stick over the green blades.

Tim could see in his mind's eye the outfitter pulling back the grass and finding the golden blonde hair and athletic frame of the lifeless volleyball player in the brush. He imagined black flies crawling and swarming over her eyes and nostrils and a stink hitting like a sucker-punch that would cause him to void his stomach at the girl's feet.

Instead, the searcher bent and rose from the grass with something in his hand. Something long and white. A bone. It swayed in the man's hand as he walked towards the group and Tim's mind swam to a place where he'd seen one like it before.

"What's that?" Bob Larson, the math teacher, asked in a near-whisper.

"It's a jawbone," Pender said.

Bob went white. "From the girl?"

"From a cow," Pender clarified with an annoyed tone. "A cow elk."

He presented it to the group and showed them the L-shaped bone, which still held a few teeth similar to those Merv had found. "The rest of it is back there," he told them, cocking his head in the direction of the grass.

"I'm gonna call you cow whisperer, Merv," Pender said, smiling and tossing the bone at Merv's feet. He appeared to enjoy the drama he had created.

Larson stared down at the jaw and teeth for a while as everyone else slowly moved on.

"You did the right thing," Tim said quietly as the group spread out again into the pines.

"I feel stupid," Merv muttered as they headed into a ravine.

"Don't! You found more than anyone else."

"You think someone killed that elk?"

Tim shrugged. "Maybe. Why?"

"You remember how those cows were showing up dead last fall?"

***

Two months after Tim started work at Meadowlark High School he caught Merv and Jim Cooley clandestinely passing a cell phone around to some of the other kids in his class. Their zit-pocked brows rose in surprise at whatever they were seeing on the screen and their jaws dropped. Tim quietly strode towards them, wondering if it would be porn. Instead, the screen showed four hooves jutting skyward from a bloated black lump.

"What's that?" he asked.

Merv quickly snapped the cell phone closed and dropped it onto his lap. "Sorry, Mr. Ross."

"Really, it's cool, Merv. I'm just curious what that thing is."

The boys, who were supposed to be helping each other memorize Hamlet's soliloquy, exchanged nervous looks.

"I'm not going to take the phone away or anything. You go hunting or something?" he asked, doubting that these two *World of Warcraft* fanatics ever left their basements, let alone went out hunting.

"They found a dead cow over by Roberts Lane," Merv said.

Tim frowned. "That's a big deal?"

Merv looked at Jim as if to consult him and then flipped his phone open and flashed a photo at Tim.

He saw rigid legs pointing straight up, as if the cow was imitating a cartoon drawing of a dead one. Then Merv skipped to the next picture. A close-up. The cow's lips had been cut away high along the gum line, with surgical precision. The creature's long teeth were exposed like dentures in the skull.

"They even cut off her..." Jim pointed at his crotch. "We tried to take a picture, but Yates told me to go away."

The next picture was of Captain Yates holding a coil of police line tape in one hand and waving the amateur photographer off with the other.

"This happen a lot here?" Tim asked.

"Not since my parents were kids," the boy replied. "They said when they were kids it happened and no one would go out at night."

Tim read an article about the incident in *The Meadowlark Call* the next day. Apparently the animal had had its "blood sucked out through no apparent wound."

The shadowy image crawled into his brain of a backwoods drifter kneeling on the neck of a dead cow and carving away its lips with a bowie knife by the light of a full moon. The creep's grin matched the cow's gruesome smile as he sliced away to the sound of his own raspy breathing.

Was it a joke? An elaborate, painstaking, prank? A threat? What did "they" do with the parts that had been taken?

How do you learn to do something like that and so well without getting caught?

***

"Mr. Ross," Merv whispered in the growing darkness of the ravine, "I went up to the cabin where they found Heather. It's just down the mountain a ways, and there was a devil worshiper sign there."

"A what?"

"You know, like an upside-down star with a circle."

"Yeah?"

"Can I ask you something?" the kid hissed, stopping to face his teacher.

"Sure."

"Do you think devil worshipers are taking over?"

"What?"

"My youth pastor said that they start by sacrificing animals and then take over whole towns—the police, mayors, everybody, until everyone is doing it and nobody has a choice."

"I'll have to start going to church again if it's gotten that interesting."

"He says they drink the blood of virgins, and that was what they did to Heather Brady."

You think Heather Brady was a virgin? Tim thought, thankful he hadn't said it out loud.

"I bet that's why we can't find Cassidy Heintz."

"I don't think that all adds up, Merv," Tim said, turning back to his search. "Why would Yates's niece be gone if he had been part of this Devil cult?"

"So people won't suspect him of being part of it."

Tim stared at the kid in the half dark of the narrow ravine. Again, he saw that look of ashen fear that was becoming all too common in Meadowlark Valley.

"Merv, sometimes everyday people do horrible things." The image of the woman looking at him through his rifle's sights flashed in his mind.

"Who would do something like *that*, though?"

Tim frowned. "Probably the most seemingly normal person you'd ever meet." Tim immediately wished he hadn't said that because the kid's expression turned from a look of fear to a look of something like suspicion. He turned and walked deeper into the ravine, feeling Merv's eyes on him.

Who would do something like that?

Tim followed the trickle of a thin stream as the ravine narrowed and darkened.

A better question would be why didn't any of us do something to stop it?

He thought about Mr. Carson fuming in their corner of the teachers' lounge after Heather Brady's body had been found in that cabin back last spring.

"It's typical," Carson spat.

"Did you know her?"

"That little girl?" the old man replied, as if Brady had been a happy pigtailed kid jumping rope in saddle shoes. The old man nodded.

"I had her come and talk with me every day for a while. Wild and confused and mercurial as all get out," Mr. Carson's seventy-year-old voice had crackled through his thin frame like cellophane or an old phonograph. "But being confused and crazy and making bad choices as a fourteen-year-old girl is no excuse for her to end up dead and who knows what else before those Alan boys found her Saturday."

Mr. Carson set his bottle of orange juice down and frowned at it. "We used to look out for each other here, used to have a community where nothing like that would have happened."

In the ravine Tim stopped to probe the underbrush that had thickened in the narrowest part of the crevice.

It wasn't my fault.

Tim thrust the walking stick he had been issued into the ferns, prodding and turning the dowel as the team had been briefed to do in case the Heintz girl might be unconscious in the brush. Tim wondered if each thrust into the leaves might stir up a Nike-clad foot or the pale flesh of a half-buried hand in the black earth.

A former version of Tim wouldn't have been able to jab at a thicket for the body of a lost girl so nonchalantly. That change had begun when he saw Gilmore shot and bleeding to death as they waited for the chopper.

A week after Gilmore died, their nine-man squad of badly shaken carpenters and electricians had found themselves taking fire once more. Everyone had shouted and shot high in response and hoped the usual show of noise and movement would, as Tim's drill sergeant had mockingly put it, "Make the bad men go away." That was the time that Tim had laid as still as a snake under the front fender of a Humvee and, forcing all the air out of his lungs, carefully placed his sights over an upstairs window where he had seen the muzzle flash. He blocked out every former impulse and teaching he'd received as a child about "not hitting," about "being nice," and "thou shalt not kill" as he slowly felt the growing weight of his index finger tip squeeze the trigger. Then he had heard the bang and saw a figure lurch in the shadows of that window.

Tim was still thankful that he didn't see the man's face—not very well, anyway. A tall guy with curly black hair and beard had appeared from the shadows, clutching his chest as his AK dropped. His head slammed against the concrete of the window sill before he fell out of sight. Even in the distance Tim could see the patch of blood the shooter had left on the window's frame.

He remembered it being around two in the morning after

he'd killed that man that he came to the vague realization that he still had the plastic spork of his MRE in his hand and the food pouch he'd opened around five o'clock the previous evening still sitting there untouched between his ankles.

Everyone seemed to know what he had done, but instead of thanking him or slapping him on the back or maybe even yelling at him for some infraction that the army loved to make up, they just glanced at him from the corners of their eyes. He had become a real bona fide killer in the midst of support troops who still thought they could win a war with plumb bobs and framing hammers.

Like all soldiers, they'd been trained to shoot enemies as far out as three hundred meters and to sing cadences about dropping napalm on children. They had adopted a whole new lexicon of battle-ready profanity and slang, but they were not *real* killers. Underneath their sawdust-specked uniforms and blemishless body armor they were still kids raised on *Rugrats* and Lunchables, far divorced from what Tim had become in the pulling of that trigger.

There were no high-fives, no bloodthirsty comments. All the secondhand war stories they had swapped, along with talk of one day "juicing" someone when they weren't framing tent platforms, had just been bluster and bravado that fell short when they saw what it really involved. Tim had fired a well-aimed round at a hodgie in a window. They left him alone in the dark with an MRE of uneaten vegetarian ratatouille.

Becoming the construction squad's first unofficial go-to killer, sacrificing his soul and former self for the good of the rest, didn't save everyone, though. It didn't save Gomez, the tiny Mexican. A round ripped right through the lower part of his face, knocking him onto the concrete. He spasmed and writhed in a scrum of Kevlar and camo that tried to save him before what remained of his mouth gaped open and his brown eyes froze on a faraway point in the sky.

Killing people didn't save Red. The six-foot-four football player from North Dakota limped up to Tim after an explosion. A hunk of gleaming steel stuck out of his thigh like an awkward and painful erection.

"Get down," Tim had barked as the pop of gunfire started across the street. Tim had crouched over his friend and fired his weapon at the hodgies attempting to flank the squad. When the shooting stopped Tim reached down to drag his friend away to a safer spot, but Red lay in a pool of his own blood that had mixed with the dusty grime of the concrete. The metal had moved during the firefight and sliced his femoral artery.

Now in the ravine Tim could hear the other searchers' footfalls and bushwhacking fading as they left him behind. In the darkness he felt something heavy inside him swell and break.

He would have given anything to go back to the Military Entrance Processing Station in Phoenix, where a surly fed had barked at him when he couldn't make the print-reader scan his finger to sign his contract right away. If he could have done so, he'd flip him off and walk right out the door—a free man who would never know what it would be like to become this messed up. Tim fell to his knees in the forest and sobbed.

Resignation had become the armor that insulated him from the guilt and failures and violence he'd played a crucial hand in, keeping him safe from the fatal "what ifs" of Iraq. *Had I done it that way, or done it this way, or done it sooner, would so-and-so still be alive? Or did I really need to kill that one?* They had been split-second decisions with eternal consequences. Forcing Tim to surrender any concept of right and wrong and replace it with a fatalistic belief that what would be, would be, and there was no fighting it. He had shut off whatever he needed to so he could survive.

CHAPTER 10

Tim started down the mountain around four p.m. and returned to his car. When he had enough bars on his cell he called Abbey from the road leading to town.

"What's up?" Abbey asked.

"I'm coming back into town. We were trying to find that girl," Tim explained, squinting ahead in disbelief. Ahead, a herd of cattle was being driven across the road from one pasture to another by a woman on horseback and a fat man on an ATV.

"They were talking about her at work. Anything?"

"I don't think so." Tim stopped to let the cows pass, wondering if it was still normal for animals to be driven cowboy-style across public roads. "My group didn't find anything anyway," he continued, "but when I was up there I started thinking about the other girl that disappeared."

"Heather Brady," Abbey clarified. "I heard about that even at UW."

"Yeah." Tim leaned back in his seat as the cattle trotted and bobbed over the oil-slicked road. "It just started to bother me why I let that girl sit in my class last year and never tried to help her."

"How could you have helped her? They still don't know who did it."

A calf split from the herd and made a hard left between Tim's car and the ditch, apparently deciding it didn't want to be part of the group.

"I could tell she had problems. I should have taken her aside and just talked to her. I could have at least tried to get her to trust me a little, maybe say something about what was really going on."

The woman on horseback sprang from the ditch and cut between Tim's Subaru and the errant bovine, leading it back to the herd.

"You do know that single guys, really any guys, should be careful about getting involved in an unstable teenage girl's life," Abbey cautioned.

Two runny cowpies had been left in the road as the last of the cattle crossed the ditch.

"I still should have tried something, though. Got another teacher involved. I dunno. The messed-up part is that I didn't even try—the thought didn't even really occur to me like it would have years ago."

The fat man on the ATV swatted the last cow through the opening and pulled the wire gate shut, giving Tim a two-fingered wave.

"What happened to that girl happened because a bad person did something terrible," Abbey said. "It wasn't because of what you did or didn't do. Look, I'm about to take a break. Why don't you come by my work for a bit?"

***

The sign reading *Meadowlark Valley Animal Clinic* was flanked by pictures of two happy dogs atop a long white trailer parked in a backyard. Tim pulled up where the gravel drive terminated at the edge of the grass growing around the building. Abbey came down the ramp from the front door, beaming in a pair of teal scrubs.

"Hey! How was beating up on yourself all afternoon?"

Tim grinned in spite of himself. "Good. Not my best work, though."

"I just wanted to stare at you creepily for a minute and then fantasize about you for the rest of the day until we can be together again." She grinned and made a show of looking Tim up and down with overdramatic lechery.

"Sure there isn't something more you want to do to me?"

Abbey laughed. "Maybe if you're really good and quit being hard on yourself we can figure something out."

"That's the best incentive I've ever been given."

Abbey took Tim by the hand and led him towards the creek that ran behind the clinic. "Seriously, though, I wish telling you that you are my little brother's hero and that he's crazy about you would be enough for you to feel redeemed," she sighed.

"Him and the dog, right?"

"And me," Abbey said, looking up at Tim with an earnestness that cut right through him.

"You're crazy about... me?" Tim asked hesitantly, expecting a cruel punchline.

Abbey's expression remained dead serious. Then she offered a quick smile, "Not like in a Sharon Stone stalkery kind of way, but yeah. I haven't met anyone like you, Tim."

Tim shook his head in disbelief.

"Tim, have I messed something up?"

"No," he said quickly. "But... even after what I told you about that woman in Iraq you're still crazy about me?"

"Tim, I don't make out with just anyone," she said in mock offense.

"It's not just about making out then?"

"No. You aren't that good, anyway," she said dryly.

"What?"

"I'm kidding," she responded, grinning. "Yer a good maker-outer, but I think you have a lot more potential than just that."

They stared at the falling seeds of the cottonwood turning to gold over the creek in the setting sun.

Tim took a deep breath. "Abbey, I really, really, really, like you!"

"Wow!" she exclaimed, laughing, "I really, really, really like you, too."

"I haven't really talked to anyone—I mean, really talked to anyone since before I left."

"I can tell." She smiled sadly. "You should. I don't think this disengaged person you worry about being is who you really are. Listen, I have to go back to work. Why don't you go see what David's up to? I'm off at seven tonight and then we can watch a movie or something together."

***

As his car roared down the road to Abbey's house that evening, the low sunlight gave every blade of grass a yellow laser edge and made the dropping cottonwood pods glow like falling stars. Tim couldn't believe that someone as great as Abbey could be real.

A killer of women, an automaton who had looked the other way when a girl was being lured to something terrible, a nervous creature who jumped when people greeted him. A husk of a human still tormented by memories of gunfire and blood that encroached on his everyday life. Yet this goddess knew his worst secret *and still really, really, really liked him!*

Tim pulled up to David and Abbey's place and knocked on the door.

"What are you up to?" Tim asked when the kid answered.

"I'm playing *The Sims*," he said as he let Tim into the house.

"Wanna watch a movie or play some Xbox till Abbey gets back?"

Hanging out with David didn't seem so weird now that Tim was dating his sister.

"Check this out," David said, leading Tim to the kitchen table where a cardboard mailing tube had been opened. David spread a rolled poster over the table. It showed a shaven-headed man with a square jaw and sunken cheeks rappelling into the frame from a helicopter and pointing an M-4 carbine at the camera.

"The recruiter I talked to on the phone sent it to me," David said with a grin.

"When he isn't killing Al Qaeda he probably works for Calvin Klein," Tim observed skeptically of the GI Joe before him.

"You don't like it?" David asked.

"Nah, it's cool, but people always seem to think soldiers are supermen, when most of them are just regular guys."

David studied Tim, not quite sure what he meant.

"Anyway, what do you want to do?"

"Abbey said you have a bunch of the *X-Files*. Can we watch those?"

The duo drove over to Tim's house where season two of the *X-Files* still lay on the coffee table after the other night.

"Whatever one you want to watch," Tim said as he walked to the kitchen, poured food into Grover's bowl and topped off her water. He came back and found the kid had laid all the DVDs from season one out on the coffee table where he read the back sleeves.

"I'm trying to find out which episodes are about ghosts," the boy explained.

"Search away."

Tim picked up a copy of *American Rifleman* and sat on his recliner. He didn't want to watch a show about ghosts, and didn't really want the kid to. He felt that trying to stop him would be admitting that there might be something to fear.

He had made it almost all the way through an article about Rossi's mini ranch rifle before he heard David finally load a disc into the DVD tray. The episode followed phantoms haunting a nursing home and Tim couldn't figure out how such fuzzy special effects and the predictable bickering between Mulder and Scully had ever seduced everyone back in the 1990s.

David was rapt, though, his eyes wide as if receiving a revelation in a born-again church.

You would think such a tech-smart kid, one who wasn't a bad writer himself, would struggle to relate to such a clunky old program…

Skimming through the gun magazine and then growing bored, Tim tried to watch the awful show. He could see the boy's eyelids were starting to droop. When they finally closed, Tim stopped the DVD and went into the kitchen to make a turkey sandwich. After covering the turkey and mustard with a cap of bread, an ear-splitting scream issued from the living room. Tim crouched, the butter knife half covered in mayonnaise wrapped tightly into his fist with the small blade protruding outward. Grover bounded off of her bed. Tim shot into the living room.

David sat ramrod straight on the couch. His eyes were doing their best to pop from their sockets and his mouth still gaped from the scream. Tim scanned the room left to right then back again, his fists up and his knife ready. The space was empty and the door secure. He looked back at the kid whose already pale skin had gone deathly white, like an old tombstone.

"David?"

The boy wouldn't look at him.

"Dave, did you have a nightmare?"

The boy's eyes flitted around the room. He seemed confused. Tim tried to force a reassuring grin. "You had a bad dream."

David continued to look around in shock.

"Everybody has nightmares, it's no big deal," Tim said, though the phrase hit a little too close to home.

David nodded absently, though his big eyes where still focused on something very far away.

"You remember what happened?" Tim asked.

"Uh-huh."

"What?"

The boy shook his head and stared down at his feet.

"Pretty bad, huh? Listen, Dave," Tim said softly, "you're okay!"

The boy shook his head.

"Come on, David, what's going on?"

The boy took a deep breath before making eye contact with Tim. "I know what happened to Cassidy Heintz."

CHAPTER 11

"How do you know what happened to her?" Tim asked. "Did someone say something? Were you there when something happened?"

"I saw her," David said, shaking his head and looking sick.

"When?"

"When I fell asleep."

It would have been simple to tell the boy something like "it was just a dream," but something about him, something about how he reacted, seemed to run thicker and deeper than a kid having a nightmare.

"Is she okay?" Tim asked, trying to hide his skepticism.

"She's in an abandoned house along the Green River. She's dead."

Tim plumbed the boy's eyes and saw the familiar look of terror he'd seen that last week of school. David's fear was so convincing it threatened to drag Tim back there again and he had to look away and compose himself for a second.

"I guess we better go see, then," Tim said, half joking.

David shook his head. "You don't want to see it, Mr. Ross."

"David, we'll go out wherever you think she is and I can tell you right now nothing will be out there. They're just dreams, man. I have them, too." Tim said, thankful that he could sound so certain, because truthfully he was trying just as hard to convince himself as he was the boy.

"When we find her out there, then will you believe me?"

Tim laughed. "If we find her where you say she is, I'll give you my gun collection," he said, rising from the couch eager to prove to himself as much as to David that none of it was real. "Let's go." He swatted David jovially on the leg hoping his bravado would overcome the glimmer of uncertainty that rested on him.

He led the reluctant kid out of the house to his car. As Tim stuck the key into the ignition David took his spot in the passenger seat. He still looked scared.

"David, back in Iraq we had this disgusting old sergeant major, just mean and crazy, but one time before we went on a mission he said, 'When you think the Devil is out there be sure to grin, because half the time he isn't even there and if he is, nothing good ever comes from being a... uh... *wussy*,'" Tim told him, toning the original quote down somewhat.

"What's that mean?"

"It means either there's nothing to be scared of or, if there is, being afraid won't help."

"Do you think I'm a wussy?"

"No," Tim said honestly as he pulled into the street and drove away from the house. "No, I think you're scared, like me and everybody else. You're just more honest about it."

"Sounds like a wussy."

"A wuss is someone who's scared and fails to act when he should. The rest of us are scared, but we still do what we have to if we need to," Tim said catching the boy's eyes in the low green light of the car's gauges. "That's the difference."

Tim didn't want a repeat of what had happened at the gun range and promised himself that if the kid got too scared they'd turn around. He told himself that what he was doing could be good for the kid, showing him there was nothing to be frightened of, but he wouldn't admit to himself that he was trying to extinguish his own fears about he and the kid having the same nightmares.

Watching the broken yellow line fly at them in the headlights as they left the lights of town behind, Tim wished he could go back to having simple teenage fears. To a time when nightmares were spawned by Hollywood's juvenile efforts, not by the cold realities of IEDs, snipers, and a shrieking woman holding the dangling, bloody remains of her child. Tim would love to be scared by the innocuous and nostalgic again—to the hoary old campfire tales that bonded Cub Scouts in the darkness of the woods or the scares that made the pretty girl you had been staring at during a Halloween party finally move next to you and grab your hand in the televised glow of *The Amityville Horror*.

"One time sophomore year, me and some of my buddies went and peed on a statue of this woman in the cemetery by our high school. We called her Yellow Mary, kind of like Bloody Mary. People said after you did it, you were supposed to walk away ten steps and then when you turned back she would have moved."

"Did it work?" David asked.

"Of course it worked," Tim said. "You're stumbling around in the dark with your friends, half drunk, and then after you walk away the light plays tricks on your mind and you already have a pre-suggestion. Then, sure enough, you start debating with your spooked-out friends in the dark about whether or not she moved and then like a mob of idiots you all decide she did."

"You have to turn here," David said, pointing to the left.

"I really think this is all in your head, Dave. Just like that statue."

At least that was what he hoped.

They cruised past the low sagebrush-studded flats outside town.

"There'll be a right-hand turn somewhere up here," the boy said, peering into the blackness. Tim slowed down and after crawling along the blacktop, saw a gap in the brush on the shoulder. He pulled off the pavement onto a road deeply rutted into the gray clay, the headlights making the sage growing from the middle of the track appear surreal and ominous in the dark, like the claws of half-buried zombies or witches' fingers reaching for the moon.

"How do you know where we are going?" Tim asked as they continued through the night, the weeds making tinny pinging noises against the undercarriage.

"There's an old house out here everyone says is haunted. It's what I saw in my dream."

The car negotiated an awkward dip into a gully and then, as it climbed out, the headlight beams crawled up the facade of a ranch house by the bank of the Green River. The fondant-like adobe had half fallen away, showing crudely placed blocks of sandstone with fat gaps between them where the mortar had disintegrated. Four windows, two upstairs and two downstairs, were set deep in the thick walls like sunken eyes staring back from a bleached skull. An open doorway on the ground floor between the two bottom windows looked like a puckered mouth.

It was nearly enough to make Tim reconsider his plan, but he looked over at David and cleared his throat. "You ready for this?"

The boy was clearly frightened, but he steeled himself and nodded as he stared at the building in front of them.

Teacher and student arrested in abandoned house late at night. Tim pictured the headline. It might be the end of his career if they were caught trespassing in the old place. But it wasn't just the fear of getting caught that made Tim so reluctant to go in there.

We'll go in, we'll come out and we'll both be better off!

He turned off the headlights and blackness spread over everything like a layer of mud.

Tim exited the car, clicked on his flashlight, and began striding over the crusty parched clay. To his relief he heard the car door open and close behind him as the boy followed.

They walked up to the house, skirting the sagebrush that attempted to reclaim the path once well-trodden by who knew how many boots and horseshoes. Odd bits of wire and a rusted tin can lay partially submerged in the caliche-like dirt.

The front door to the house hung out from its bottom hinge like a broken bat wing. The pair stopped on the threshold and needled shafts of light into the bowels of the old place from their flashlights. The silence was almost reverential as they listened for any sound. It almost felt like the house was listening back. A spindle-legged chair with a broken back stood on the rough-hewn floorboards of the hall. Tim half-expected to see some forlorn figure from a hundred years ago to materialize upon it and glare back at them as intruders.

"Where's the girl?" Tim whispered, fearing that if he raised his voice it would violate the stillness of this old place.

"I really think we should go," the boy whispered back nervously.

"Dave, if you are able to deal with this you might not have so many bad dreams."

The long hallway swallowed the probing beam of Tim's flashlight, making him doubt the truth of his own words.

"There," the boy squeaked, his voice thin and reedy in the dark as the shaft of light fixed on a closed door at the far end of the hall. "That's what I saw."

Tim took a quick glance backward in the direction of the car and the night sky beyond. The stars were visible now, like pinpricks of burning magnesium through black felt. He thought

of other times he had stood outside crumbling ancient edific-
es and had hazarded a glance over his shoulder at the world
outside, thinking it might be the last thing he'd ever see. He
recalled a ruined Iraqi econo-car, a lone streetlight humming
over a sand-blown street, a dog barking somewhere.

Tim flexed his hand, wishing for the pistol grip of his M-16
to kiss it, wishing to be mashed again between the sweating
bodies of his squad in "the stack;" a human centipede of sweat-
stained Kevlar that would kick open a flimsy door and slither
into someone else's world, pointing weapons high and low,
terrified and itching to pull their triggers.

Tim took another long, slow, breath and raised his Maglite
above his shoulder, holding it close to the bulb so he could
swing it down swiftly like a police baton on anything that
might assail him or David. Then he stepped inside.

The cool air in the house smelled salty from the alkali. The
heads of square nails had worked their way just above the
surface of the flooring like mouse turds caught in the roving
flashlight beam. Thankfully the boards didn't pop or snap under their weight like some old floors would. Scanning left to
right he watched the dust motes dance in the flash beam. He
cursed when he saw there were two other doorways branching
out from the hall.

They made them instantly vulnerable. Entering a suspect
building was dangerous, but to have a doorway on either side
of you was the worst. Out of instinct he stopped at the corner
of the right door and swept his light inside the room to his left.

The beam revealed a huge stone fireplace at the far side of
the room, with a broken mirror over it. He wondered vaguely
about when that mirror had last reflected anything other than
the room in front of it. A table and some overturned chairs
were scattered nearby, but Tim saw no apparent threat. He

scanned the room to his right, void except for an assortment of bottles next to a shredded mattress on the floor. Layers of illegible graffiti had been keyed into the soft plaster walls.

Advancing toward the ominously closed door at the far end of the hall, Tim risked a glance back at David. He looked even more ghostly white, his eyes like bulging golf balls in the dark. Tim reached down and touched the low round knob of the door. Its patina of rust felt like sandpaper. If ever there would be a time to encounter some undiscovered abomination this would be the perfect place. The knob made a grinding sound as he twisted it and he felt a flash of hope that maybe it would be locked or jammed, but the door moved inward, groaning on its rusted hinges, the sound echoing off the stone walls around them.

Tim held his breath in the darkness. He didn't want to believe any of the kid's delusions, but in a place like this it was hard not to cringe at the sound. He braced himself to face whatever fang-toothed, swift-clawed, death-dealing legions might have been aroused by the noise.

The door swung open wider and he saw that they were standing at the top of a flight of steps leading down into darkness. Tim pointed his beam of light downwards but could see very little of where they might lead to.

"You can wait here if you want," he whispered before taking a tentative step onto the first rocky stair. He pointed his light further down the stairway and now saw it ended in a dirt floor not far below. He took another very slow step downward. To his surprise, he heard David step down after him and together they descended till they reached the bottom. Tim kept his light raised, ready to slam it down on anything that might rush at them from the darkness.

The basement had the cloying smell of dirt and something

else lingering in the dampness. Rags and the heavy burlap of gunny sacks were scattered everywhere on the floor. Otherwise, the space was empty except for a rusted oil drum in the corner.

Tim exhaled and shifted his grip on the light, conscious of the layer of sweat between his hand and its checked grip. He looked back at David, hoping to see the face of a boy who had just slain a dragon. Instead his eyes were locked on the oil drum.

Tim followed his gaze hesitantly, then approached the drum and gave it a swift kick to assure the kid that the room was all clear. The drum didn't budge at Tim's kick. Instead, it gave the dull thud of something heavy and full.

It'll just be potatoes, or trash, or a giant stash of used pornography. Shoot, it might even be an oil drum actually full of oil.

The reassuring thoughts really didn't help much as he shone the light onto the rusted lid of the drum and gingerly lifted it with the tip of his fingernail. He sniffed as a faint smell wafted out. Just a trace, but it was enough to call back the memory of the awful gut-puking, rolling stench he'd smelled too many times before, the fragrance exuded by the bloated, gray-green corpses he'd seen in the streets of Iraq as the dogs descended to eat their eyes, noses and ears.

Tim covered the lower part of his face with a hand and kicked the barrel over. He knew that whatever was in there was dead, but he needed to know if it really was what he suspected. The lid rolled off and a new looking green trash bag wrapped with fresh, gray duct tape spilled halfway out of the rusty old thing. The smell hit like a tidal wave.

"Get out!" Tim shouted as he turned and pushed the boy up the stairs.

CHAPTER 12

Tim called the police the moment they were out of the house. It was only as he and David waited for them to arrive that he realized that he might have wanted to talk with an attorney first.

Officer Farner arrived around nine p.m. and found the body still lying on the floor where the unlikely pair had left it. He squatted down and cut open the green trash sack with the lock-back Buck knife his wife had given him for Christmas. The stench came out even stronger, making him vomit as he stared down at the bloodstained and filthy blonde hair of the volleyball player who had been missing now for fifty-one hours and twenty-seven minutes.

Later that night, Farner escorted Tim to Meadowlark's Town Hall, which also housed the Fire Department and Police Station. He handed the teacher a cup of coffee before sitting down opposite him in what looked like a break room. Captain Yates waited in the lobby outside with David and a very upset Abbey.

Farner found the dictaphone on his smartphone, turned it on and set it down on the table.

"This is Officer John Farner interviewing Tim Ross at the Meadowlark Municipal building. It's eleven-thirteen on August thirteenth, 2008." He looked up from the machine. "Mr. Ross, I've turned on an audio-recording device. Do you understand that you are currently being recorded and that anything you say can be used as evidence in a court of law?"

The formality surprised Tim and he swallowed nervously.

"Yes, I understand," he replied, for the benefit of the tape. "Are you arresting me?"

Farner's serious expression softened a little and he shook his head. "No, sir, we just need to know more about what you and the Jenkins kid… uh… David Jenkins," he corrected himself, glancing at the phone, "…what you and he were doing in the structure by the Green River on county road twenty-two this evening."

Well, you see I'm a serial killer and…

Tim frowned. He wasn't sure Farner or Yates would believe anything he said, but he did his best to explain it all, even including how he'd sort of taken David under his wing.

"You didn't call us when the boy said he knew where Cassidy was," the cop remarked.

"I didn't believe him," Tim explained. "I mean, what would you have told me if I'd said 'Hey, my girlfriend's little brother had a dream and we're pretty sure you can call off the search now.'"

"At this point we still would have followed it as a lead," Farner argued. "So you didn't believe David, but you drove all the way out there?"

"That kid…" Tim said, lowering his voice at the thought of David just outside the door, "…is scared all the time. He thinks he sees ghosts. I thought we'd just stroll out to the ranch house, find a whole lot of nothing, and he would see there wasn't anything to be afraid of—that his bad dreams were just bad dreams like everyone has. If I had known that there was a body out there, believe me, I would have called you!"

"The reason why we are concerned is how the whole county went out looking for her with dogs and helicopters, and got nowhere, yet you and a teenage kid were able to go straight to her, even though she was so well hidden and really far out of the way."

"So you think I hurt her?" Tim asked.

The cop regarded the table-top for a second then returned his gaze to Tim.

"Honestly, no." He sipped from his cup of coffee then set it back on the table. "If guilt was getting to me after doing something like that, an anonymous call or letter would work just fine. I don't picture you phoning us, identifying yourself, and then sticking around with the corpse until we got there, not if you had done this."

"I didn't!"

"My concern is how we account for David knowing where Cassidy was."

"I dunno about that. Are you saying he hurt her?"

"I'd be surprised if he had it in him, frankly," Farner answered, smirking.

"He doesn't!" Tim confirmed. "I don't know how to prove to you I'm not making this up, but what happened is what happened. I wish I could be there when he wakes up screaming about a winning lottery number, or whether to bet on black, but this is what happened."

Farner sat back and stopped his voice recorder. "I'm going to level with you. I was with the Tulsa Police Department before I moved up here and whenever someone went missing that we couldn't find we'd call this lady who claimed to be a psychic." The cop frowned, looking down at his smartphone. "I'm a Christian. I didn't believe in all this hoodoo nonsense, but one time she came into the police station with a red circle on a city map, saying she had dreamed about where a missing boy was. Sure enough, she led us right to that little guy's remains." He shook his head and pursed his lips briefly. "I don't know what makes things work the way they do. I always felt embarrassed about listening to her, but sometimes these dreams she claimed to have really did work out, and that was after lots of background checks." He sighed and slid his big cowboy hat off the table, then put it on as he rose. "I apologize for the inconvenience. I need your cell phone number in case we have further questions. You'd really make my day if the lab guy from Evanston could take a DNA sample from both you and the boy tomorrow."

Tim nodded as Farner slid a piece of paper across for him to write his number on. The cop thanked him and opened the door for him to go. Then he seemed to have another thought.

"If that kid has another nightmare, or a vision or whatever, of where he thinks a body is, or where a suspect might be, you'll call us first, right?"

"Will do," Tim said.

Farner handed Tim a business card with a police star foiled onto it. Tim slid the card into his pocket and carried on through the door.

Abbey and David were talking with Lieutenant Yates in the lobby. The officer looked sick and pale as he glanced at Tim. It made Tim wonder if maybe that could be why he had left his underling to conduct the interview with him.

"If you can think of anything more we should know, please tell me," Yates said to Tim.

"I will. I'm so sorry about Cassidy."

Yates nodded before putting on his hat and walking out the door, looking destroyed as he made his way to his truck in the parking lot.

Tim turned to Abbey. Her eyes were brimming with tears as well.

"I'm sorry," Tim said, worried she'd start screaming at him for taking David to see a corpse, but she stepped forward and wrapped her arms around him.

She smelled like gum and some kind of cleaner, probably

from the vet's office. He stared down at her blonde hair resting against his chest and wanted to reach up and softly run his fingers over it but he saw David staring at them.

Tim gestured at him to come over. The boy approached but stood there awkwardly until Tim slid his free arm around the kid and pulled him into the hug.

CHAPTER 13

The DNA guy came round early the next morning to Tim's house and swabbed his and David's mouths.

"Hey, look, you're Saddam!" Tim joked as the lab tech inserted what looked like a long Q-tip into the boy's mouth, reminded of the famous footage of the Iraqi dictator being swabbed by military personnel after his capture to ensure they had the right man.

"You don't know how often I hear that one," the tech said dryly as he swabbed the kid's mouth.

After the man had gone, Tim made the brother and sister pancakes and they sat drowsily around the table until David went back to sleep on the couch.

"I'm really sorry about what happened," Tim said quietly.

"I was so mad!" Abbey admitted. "The police called me to say that they had David and that they needed me present to interview him in connection with Cassidy Heintz."

"I'm really sorry," Tim repeated. "I just wanted to show him he didn't need to be afraid."

"I know," she sighed. "David told me about what happened. I guess I understand what you were doing, but if he wants to go find any more missing girls, please let the police know first—or take me, at least."

Tim nodded.

"I was just really stressed out because I didn't know what was going on and…" She stopped then looked Tim in the eye. "David is the only thing I have left after all the garbage that happened with my family."

"I just thought I was helping him. If I had known, I mean,

how often do your dreams come true?"

"I told you about how David said he saw people we think might have been relatives when he was little, but some of these things he said he saw weren't nice. Sometimes he would wake up screaming, saying someone was in his room. It didn't matter where he slept or which house we were in at the time. It stopped around the time he started kindergarten and everyone wrote it off, thinking it might have been because everything was so crazy around us growing up." She kneaded a paper napkin in her fist. "I saw this show on TV about these teenage girls in England who attracted a poltergeist. Apparently, bad ghosts like teenagers for some reason." She frowned. "I dunno. Maybe something is going on with David's hormones and that's why he's seeing things again. I've heard him scream in his sleep like he used to do."

Tim handed her a fresh napkin to replace the one she had crumpled up.

"I would love it if we could treat him with some antipsychotics or anti-hallucinogens, or whatever else might fix him, but…" Tears overflowed and rolled down her cheeks.

Tim went around to her side of the table. He thought about the other people he had seen cry and not helped, not comforted, and then he wrapped his arms around Abbey, sliding into the seat next to her and rocking her as she broke down.

"Do you know what it's like to have felt exhausted all your life?" she sobbed.

Tim nodded. "Maybe not *all* my life, but over the past few years, yeah, a little."

"I just want things to stop being crazy," she said, sniffing. "I feel like it's making me old fast and that I'll never be normal."

He looked into her blue eyes. "Well… for a weird old lady, you still have an amazing body."

"I hate you," she sobbed, but Tim felt relieved to see her laughing at the same time. Soon afterwards, she fell asleep on his shoulder as they sat in the kitchen. He picked her up gently and took her into the spare bedroom, removed her shoes and draped the blankets over her.

***

That evening Tim played *Ages of the Empires II* on the computer by the laundry room with the satisfaction that both of his favorite people in the world were asleep in his house, where he could protect them best.

As long as I keep the bedroom door closed, anyway.

He did his best to ignore that thought. It felt weird to be vulnerable with someone again, weird to care about someone. He thought that maybe he could resurrect something of his old self, the pre-war Tim who had tried to help disadvantaged trailer people after college and who had enlisted in the idealistic hope of handing candy and school books to hope-filled Iraqi children.

Someone knocked softly on the front door and Tim let the game run while he rose to answer it, with a sleepy Grover in tow. He slid the sash to the right and saw a bow-tied hipster in skinny jeans before him. He looked as out of place in the small Wyoming town as a lightning rod on a submarine.

Tim opened the door cautiously.

"Are you Tim Ross?" the young man asked.

Tim nodded.

"I'm Jackson Emmons from *The Meadowlark Call*. I'm wondering if I can interview you about what happened last night?"

Tim frowned at the stranger and gave the bowtie and skinny jeans a skeptical look. The young man's head was shaved on the sides below a pompadour-like mop of hair while a thin, well-kempt beard did its best to spread over his jaw and chin.

Tim hated journalists with a passion. He had started to hate hipsters, too, after they seemed to have taken over his generation while he risked his life in a world far divorced from man buns and ironic mustaches. Whenever he saw a member of the "leftist propaganda machine" as he called journalists in Iraq, he made sure to stare them down until they looked away. It hadn't been hard. Tall and gaunt, clutching a rifle, he glared with unblinking contempt from beneath his helmet at them. Americans, Aussies, Brits, Germans, the BBC, CNN, the *New York Post*—even the granola crowd from NPR—they all received the same treatment from Tim and his unit whenever they spotted "the real enemy."

"What's the difference between a soldier and a reporter in Iraq?" Tim asked the young man, feeling a growing anger as he remembered the fast-talking creatures who had shown up on the battlefield as if it was their personal movie set.

"Sorry?" Jackson asked politely.

"The reporter can leave whenever he wants and he gets paid a lot more." Tim gave a sour grin, happy to finally be able to tell a reporter exactly what he thought of him without the threat of some politician in the ranks going after him.

"Mr. Ross, I was in Iraq," Jackson said flatly.

"Me, too!" Tim said, feigning enthusiasm. "Except I wasn't a tourist, or a war profiteer."

Jackson pulled the sleeve of his tightly fitted shirt up his arm, exposing an off-pink scar about as thick as a permanent marker indented into the meat of his forearm near his elbow. He pulled the sleeve higher, showing a tattoo of three dog tags.

Tim felt a sinking feeling as he read the names of the dead on the reporter's arm. *PFC Elders, John. SPC White, Dylan. SSG*

Hernandez, Carlos.

"I was at Mosul," Jackson said.

"I am really, really, sorry," he said meekly.

"I don't like reporters either," Jackson admitted.

"Come inside."

Tim led Jackson through the living room, where David still slept on the couch, to the kitchen. "I'm really sorry, man! I wish I'd known." Tim whispered in the quiet of the kitchen.

Jackson shrugged. "It's kind of embarrassing to have jumped ship and be doing this now, but I needed a job."

In my defense, you also look like a hipster barista, Tim thought—but there was no way he would say that after the way he'd acted at the door.

"Water? Juice?" Tim asked, opening the fridge and pulling out a bottle of orange juice. "I wish I had something stronger for you."

Jackson shook his head. "I stay away from all that stuff now."

"Me, too," Tim said as they sat down at the kitchen table. "You doing okay?" Tim cocked his head at the arm the reporter had covered back up.

Jackson shrugged. "I wake up screaming sometimes, but…"

Tim nodded, wanting to tell Jackson that he had the same problem but didn't want to go into it all again.

"You think I can I interview you?"

"It's not a very good story," Tim warned.

"A dead girl found in a basement after a kid has a dream? Even in LA we didn't get that too often."

"How did you know about the dream?" Tim asked.

"It's what the police said."

David came into the kitchen looking groggy and oblivious to Jackson. He began to explore the contents of the fridge.

"David, this guy wants to interview you about last night. You game?" Tim asked dubiously.

David glanced up from the fridge, holding a jar of pickles. Before Tim could say, "those were in the fridge when I moved in, don't eat 'em," David said, "I think so."

"You sure?"

It was weird to see the reserved kid volunteering to actually talk to someone. Tim wondered if it would be good for him.

"Hold on, I have to check with his sister and the police," Tim said.

***

The next day, after going running, Tim picked up a copy of *The Meadowlark Call* from the pile growing in the driveway of the vacant house across the street and read the headline: "Local Boy Finds Missing Girl."

Abbey had repeatedly asked David if he "really wanted to talk about all this with a reporter" but she had relented when she saw how David really seemed to want to do it. Most kids were featured in the small town paper for football or basketball, apparently this would be David's shot at fifteen minutes of fame and he knew it. The police had said that they wanted as much coverage of the case as possible to "keep it fresh in people's minds," as if something like this would soon be forgotten in a town where everyone came to the grand opening of the new Maverick Gas Station with the same enthusiasm most people reserved for the Olympics.

The now very familiar picture of Cassidy Heintz in her volleyball uniform, along with a picture of the abandoned ranch house, appeared underneath the headline.

Tim skimmed through the first paragraph, still sweating from his run. It described the finding of the body and informed readers that prior to that "David Jenkins, 15, of Mead-owlark, Wyoming 'had a dream' identifying where the girl's body would be found."

Tim called David but received no answer so he ran over to the Jenkins place with the thin county newspaper rolled into his fist like a sprinter's baton. He banged on the door then let himself in, calling for David. The boy stumbled from his room in a pair of jeans and a t-shirt that said "byte me." His hair was still wet from a shower.

"Yer in the paper," Tim said, tossing it to him.

David perched himself on the leg of the couch and read for a while. Then the two sat down and ate Special K from glass bowls in the spotless kitchen.

"How's it feel to be famous?" Tim asked.

David shrugged. "About like before."

Tim grunted.

"Do you think it's weird I saw her?" the boy asked.

Tim studied the kid for a bit. Before, he would have hurried to reassure the kid, but that didn't seem right anymore.

"Yeah," Tim said.

"Do you think I'm weird?" the kid asked, his voice a little nervous.

Tim swallowed. "You're starting to grow on me."

"Really?"

"I'm eating breakfast with you, aren't I?"

The kid grinned. He flipped to the back of the newspaper and pointed to an ad reading "Couriers Wanted."

"They're supposed to call me back today."

"I bet you'll get it done faster than anyone else."

Tim turned the paper back to the lead article and stared at the spooky ranch house where they'd found Cassidy.

"David," he said, not sure how far he wanted to take it, "what exactly happens when you have one of those dreams?"

The boy stopped chewing mid-crunch and hesitated before finishing his bite. "I go to sleep."

Tim rolled his eyes. "No, like, what do you see?"

David set his spoon down on the tabletop. "It sort of depends on the dream and what happens." He looked up at Tim, a little embarrassed. "I do think some of them are just... bad dreams like anybody has. I don't always need to be asleep to see these people either."

"Are you seeing them right now, like, walking around?" Tim asked, indicating the whole kitchen, as if it were coursing with legions of the dead.

David shook his head. "Not here. I get... feelings when I see them, too. And usually I just kind of *know* what is going on. You ever had a dream where for some reason you just know something, but nothing in the dream tells you why?"

Tim nodded.

"When I saw Cassidy point to that basement door in my dream I knew we would find her down there. Then the dream kind of jumped to someone pushing her body into the barrel."

The warm morning air in the trailer seemed to grow chill and the hair on Tim's arms pricked up. The boy watched him shiver and then grinned as for the first time in their friendship David now enjoyed introducing Tim to something new and uncomfortable.

"The worst part is... sometimes I see what happens before they died," David added. "Also, I don't think everyone I see dies. I think some people just get hurt real bad or are real scared and it leaves something behind that I sort of replay."

Tim studied David not wanting to believe that this simple, quiet kid could have ever seen something like what had happened to Cassidy.

"I'm really sorry, David." Tim frowned down at the clean but scratched table-top. He had had the grotesque and abominable seared forever into his brain in Iraq, but at least when it happened he had eight other guys in his squad with him. This boy had faced horror alone.

"You're starting to believe me now, aren't you?" David speculated, not with pride—it was just a statement of fact tinged with sadness.

"Yeah," Tim said honestly.

"You know Jennifer, that story I wrote about the girl being killed at the gun range?"

"Yes."

"It wasn't just a rumor."

Before Tim could respond, an electric snap like the sound of a bug zapper disturbed the still of the tiny kitchen.

"Doorbell," David explained, rising and going to the door.

Tim saw from the corner of his eye a very big man with hulking shoulders and thick jowls filling the doorway. He had seen this kind of guy before at parent-teacher conferences and the grocery store. The word cowboy was too far removed, too romantic to describe these people. He belonged to an army of wind-burned, tired-eyed men in worn ball caps and ragged blue jeans who spent their lives pitching hay off the back of pickups in flying snow and burning red in summer saddles as they moved their cattle to greener pastures in the Uintas.

The man who filled the doorway wore an expensive-looking button-down cowboy shirt, new wrangler jeans that had gleaming copper-colored threads down the seams, and clean boots. His thick, sausage-like hands were curled meekly over the brim of a cowboy hat. His wide shoulders sagged forward like a horseshoe around his neck.

"Are you David?" the big man asked.

David nodded.

"I'm Cassidy's grandfather. Melvin Heintz."

David just stared at him.

"Come in!" Tim shouted from the kitchen as David didn't seem to understand what he was supposed to do. "Come on in!"

Tim ushered the big man into the living room. Heintz nodded his thanks as Tim gestured to a chair.

"We're very sorry about what's happened," Tim said.

The rancher nodded again and his long, busted fingernails scraped at something imaginary on his hat brim.

"I was wondering if I could ask yer boy a little more about Cassidy?" he said, not looking up from the hat.

"He's not really *my* boy," Tim explained. "I'll call his sister, but I think it'll be all right. Come on over here, David," he gestured to the teenager, pointing to the sofa opposite the old man. "You okay with talking about what you saw?"

David seemed to think about it for a moment. "He won't believe me," he said, shrugging.

"Just talk to him!" Tim turned back to Cassidy's grandfather. "Mr. Heintz, I've known David for nearly a year. He's a good student and never in any trouble. I don't know for sure how he knew where your granddaughter was, but I know he had nothing to do with what happened to her."

The old man nodded, still staring at the immaculate carpet.

"I'll be in the next room," Tim said as he grabbed his cell from the kitchen table. He went into David's room, where he sat in front of the kid's computer and bounced a text out to Abbey.

Tim didn't want to be too far away from where the boy and the man were. The old man had looked broken, grief-stricken, apparently trying to fill the horrific gap created by all the unanswered questions. However, if he did decide the boy knew something more than he was telling, Tim wanted to be ready to stop him from hurting David.

"The police said that you are supposed to see things in visions or something?" he heard Heintz asked in a hushed tone.

Silence.

"Yes, sir," David admitted very softly.

"Did you see who…" The old man took a breath, "…who hurt Cassidy like this?"

"I saw a man hurting her. He had his hands around her throat and she was trying to push him away."

Tim winced, knowing that Cassidy's grandpa must be doing the same.

"Do you know him?" Melvin Heintz asked. It was a pretty normal question in a small town where everyone knew everyone.

"No, I didn't see his face."

"You sure?"

A magpie shot past the window shrieking as it flew away towards the distant buttes. Silence.

"Son, I really need to know who could have hurt her like this." The old man's voice shook.

"If I knew, I would have told Yates. I would have given them an artist sketch even, but I never saw the guy's face. I'm really sorry," David added.

Tim walked in past the living room under the guise of getting some more cereal. He studied the big rancher, whose eyes were flooded with tears.

"Son," he said, leaning in, "if you do figure out who did this I want you to tell me first, okay?"

Tim pretended to rifle through the cupboards for something as he watched Melvin reach into his shirt pocket and slide something from it into David's hand.

"That's my number," the old man said, pointing to whatever he had handed the kid.

David turned up his palm and stared at it.

"Just call me and give me their name."

Then the big man rose, whipped his sleeve across his eyes, and left, sliding his hat on as he descended the wooden steps into the front yard.

Carrying a reloaded bowl of cereal, Tim straddled the arm of the sofa next to David. A yellow post-it note with a tack and feed store's logo printed at the top rested in David's palm. A phone number had been written across its middle. Underneath the post-it lay a thin wad of twenty-dollar bills fastened with a paperclip.

David held the cash up to the light as if he didn't believe it were real.

"What's this?" he asked.

"I'm not sure," Tim said, trying to remember if there had been a reward offered for information about the girl. He didn't think he had heard of one.

"Why does he think I wouldn't tell the police if I knew more?" David asked.

Tim shook his head and slid off the arm of the couch onto its cushions. "He's upset and doing anything he can to try to fix what went wrong, I think."

David began to count the bills. "It's a hundred bucks."

"David, if you do figure out who killed that girl, tell the police first, not that guy."

"Why?"

"Because it's legal. And, honestly, if you tell Melvin first, I don't know what might happen."

"If Melvin takes care of it on his own, what's so bad about that?" David asked.

Tim couldn't answer that one for several seconds. "I guess the worst thing would be if he got the wrong guy."

CHAPTER 14

Incredibly, disgustingly, throat searingly hot. Tim didn't feel like the tough, ground-pounding killer he had become. Instead, he felt a desperate need to vacate the clay canyons he patrolled and go for a swim in the blue waters of any American swimming pool back home. That was when he realized he was dreaming again, returned like a defective product to the old recurring nightmare.

He recognized the familiar bend in the canyon and sucked hot desert air into his lungs as he rounded it.

As always, the figure hunkered down in the cave. He lowered his rifle, letting it swing from its sling, and frowned. The woman in the burqa had become a regular cast member of unwanted dreams. He felt annoyed and listless, knowing the only way he could end the horrible ritual was to approach the smiling corpse, see its gore, experience the terror, and be reminded of everything awful he had been a party to.

A breeze tugged at the woman's black shroud but she remained stock still. His eyes traveled down to the swaddled black mass in her lap. It was motionless, too.

Tim cursed.

Why was this his legacy? Why couldn't he move on? What would be so wrong with that? It had been a war, a place where bad things happened, a place where people make mistakes.

"You know what?" he said to the figure, "I'm not doing this anymore!"

He turned to walk away but saw that the curve in the canyon had been replaced by a wall of rock, as if by magic. No retreat. Had the canyon sealed itself behind his back in his other dreams or just now that he refused to submit to the horror the cave dweller required of him?

He turned back to her.

"Fine!"

He sat down in the dusty clay, crossing his legs, and eyeballed the figure. "I'll sit here all day and just ignore you. I can sleep in till the end of August when I have to go back to work."

After sweating in the heat for a while under the still gaze of the figure in the shadows he grew angry. "Screw this!" He slid forward into the prone position and brought his rifle sights up to his face.

"I'm giving you a count of three and then I want you to disappear!" he shouted from behind his weapon. "One!"

No response.

"Two!"

Nothing.

"Three!" He flicked the safety off.

The figure held as still as a gargoyle.

"You sure about this?" he challenged, though inside he was asking himself the same question. "Well, ready or not, here they come."

He pulled the trigger and gave her a three-round burst.

Pop! Pop! Pop! Three supersonic spinning rounds came screaming out of the muzzle like tiny full-metal-jacketed hornets whizzing through the air on a last fatal mission towards the center of her being.

Tim waited for her to crumple and fall. But she just sat there, as still as a shrouded Buddha.

"You bulletproof now? Yer just going to make me stand here while you pull your shroud off and make me feel like human garbage again?"

He glanced behind him and saw that the canyon remained

walled off. His left hand skimmed across his body armor as he wished he had a grenade. Instead, he felt the odd lump of something alien. He looked down and saw a bayonet. The only one he'd ever seen was one their platoon leader had strapped to his assault pack. "It was my grandfather's," was all he had said when people asked him about it, but everyone understood that he carried it like a talisman. Now its grooved brown leather handle protruded from a scabbard strapped to Tim's armor.

"Saw this in a movie once!" he whispered as he pulled the blade out and figured out how to attach it to the bayonet lug on his rifle. Then he pointed it at the woman once more.

"Let's see if you're blade-proof, too!" Tim called, not willing to think about where this nightmare was going. He eyeballed the figure past the point of his bayonet, hoping she would run, but there wasn't any movement. He surged up off the ground, his feet braced against the clay like sprinters' blocks, and then charged towards the corpse as the long blade on the end of his rifle bounced and swayed.

She didn't even flinch.

I'm going to kill you!

Twenty yards from the cave and she still held still.

Get up and run away so I don't have to do this!

Ten yards from the cave he felt the growing icebox chill of the cavern reaching out to him. Still he saw no movement from the woman.

Die! Die! Why won't you die? The old cadence's lyrics thumped in his head.

At the lip of the cave the sweat on his skin flash-froze to ice. Suddenly deafened by the noise of war—gunshots, the roaring of flames, the screams of a terrified woman, he aimed the thick blade right at her sternum, right where he had pushed the muzzle of his M-16 so hard that day in Iraq and lunged.

The figure in black gasped as the metal pierced her core with a vegetable slicing "schwick" sound and she fell backward as Tim charged over her.

He pulled the bayonet out of her torso and drove it back into her belly through the thick black fabric of the burqa. Again and again he stabbed her. Her hands slid to her belly to protect herself and his heart sank when he saw the familiar tassle-like cord extending from her fist into her sleeve, the reason that had made him do what he did that awful day in Iraq.

Pulling the blade from her body for a final time, Tim loaded up and kicked the corpse in the side of the head, dislodging her veil. He saw the face not of a mid-eastern woman or of Abbey's grey-green fleshed zombie twin, but the face of Abbey herself, not bloated or dead, but the same one he had kissed, the same one that he'd seen haloed by the setting sun shining through her hair on their first walk.

"Abbey!" Tim screamed.

Her teeth were bared in pain and her hands were clutching her bayonetted abdomen, her eyes slits of pain. The baby Tim usually saw during his nightmares never appeared.

Tim dropped his weapon and fell to his knees. The burqa was gone and Tim saw only the sundress she'd worn on their first date. Ugly slits of crimson were spreading through the silky fabric over her chest and abdomen.

Tim crushed his palms against the bloody spots where he had hurt the only person he'd loved, hoping that direct pressure would somehow close the gaping wounds. She writhed at his touch.

"I'm sorry!" he shrieked.

The warm blood spread and blossomed with the flowers on her dress as she grew pale.

He lurched forward and tilted Abbey's head back, opening

her lips and breathing into her mouth. He knew it was useless
to give mouth-to-mouth to a victim who was bleeding out, but
in the dream it seemed right, as if he could give one last part
of himself that would stay with her wherever she was going.
He forced his air into her lungs. Then she disappeared entirely
and he collapsed alone in the darkness of the cave.

***

Tim woke sobbing.

Hail smacked into the house's tin roof like golf balls, or the
gunfire in his dreams. He ran his hand over his tear-stained
cheeks and then called Abbey on his cell. It rang and rang and
Tim was sure she was dead until she picked up.

"Abbey, I'm so sorry!" he yelled into the receiver.

"Tim?" she asked drowsily.

"I'm so sorry. Are you okay?"

"Yeah." She sounded concerned. "Are you?"

"No."

"I'm coming over," she said.

Tim posted himself by the back window as Grover paced
around him nervously until a pair of headlights burned
through the hail. He ran outside in his boxers, the hailstones
bouncing off his bare skin. He opened Abbey's door and shot
an arm around her as they ran to the house. The screen door
slammed behind them and he pulled her wet hair back from
her face and stared into those blue eyes. They were still swimming with life and expression. He planted a kiss firmly and
lastingly right on her lips.

Tim felt her start in surprise and then relax and lean into him.
He squeezed her against him, holding onto her as if an earth-
quake or bomb or the end of the world might separate them.

"You're okay?" he asked again.

"This has been one of the better wake-up calls I've ever had," she said, grinning, but bemused. "You?"

He shook his head, faintly aware that the water on his face wasn't just from the rain. "You know how I said I killed a woman in Iraq?"

She nodded.

He told her in detail about the woman. About the disgusting viscera of the baby hanging down from what used to be its body, even how its organs had flopped against his bare wrist and how he had tried so hard to make the woman go away, thrusting the muzzle of his weapon at her.

"I pointed the gun at her to make her go away and she put her hand up in front of her face, holding the baby with the other one." Tim demonstrated, looking something like a Heisman trophy. "I saw she had something weird in the hand coming up out of her burqa. I thought it was a detonator and before she could do anything else I shot her in the face."

The words sounded too matter-of-fact, too blunt to be spoken in a quiet kitchen thousands of miles from a war in Iraq.

"She had a bomb?" Abbey asked.

"I saw it all in my head. A dual attack. After the first explosion, another insurgent appears among all the confusion and approaches personnel, asking for help. Once they get enough people around or get close enough to us, they blow themselves up, and you with them."

Abbey frowned.

"We'd even been given a training scenario about it. I swore as I saw that thing that she must have picked that dead baby off the ground after the blast as a diversion. The vehicle-borne IED was part of an ambush. They started shooting right after I shot that lady. I pulled back behind a vehicle and started firing back. But even during the firefight I glanced over at her at least twice, worried that a round might hit her and blow us all up. I can still see what she had in her hand as she lay there in the street."

Tim rose and disappeared into his room, not really caring if it was haunted anymore, then returned to Abbey and dropped a string of wooden beads into her hand.

"The way she held them at first all I saw were those things on the end, so they looked a lot more threatening." He pointed to three bits of string that almost looked like a tassel. "When she dropped on the ground I could see them a little better and then, later, I saw them for sale in a shop downtown. Our interpreter explained that they are some kind of prayer beads. After that I saw them everywhere, noticed them in people's hands, in shops. Usually I saw men use them, but for some reason she had a set. I just wish I could have realized what they were sooner."

Abbey's mouth was agape as she stared down at the beads in her hand. She looked up at Tim and he could see the tears welling in her eyes. She reached out and wrapped her arms around him. He didn't feel like he deserved to have anyone embracing him, but he didn't push her away.

"I'm so sorry," she whispered over the sound of the rain that had replaced the hail outside.

"I told our chaplain," Tim went on. "He told me that I had a right to self-defense, no matter what, and if I thought I needed to protect myself or other soldiers then I did the right thing."

"I think he was right, Tim."

"Tell that to her."

"I can't," she answered, looking up at him. "Neither can you. Killing yourself isn't going to bring her back. It isn't going to help her or me or David."

Tim stared at her. "Why did you say I was going to kill myself?"

"I know what it's like to feel terrible," she said. "Sometimes you can just tell."

They held each other in the dark for a while, listening to the thud and patter of the storm.

"I had a nightmare that I hurt you, like I didn't know it was you until it was too late," he told her. "I think that has been the worst dream I've had since the ones about things that really happened."

"If you hurt me," Abbey said severely, "I'll send my little brother after you."

Tim laughed in spite of himself and Abbey smiled.

"I think maybe the dream is because I feel guilty about what I did and that somehow I don't deserve you, like I'm worried I'll ruin your life like I've done to my own."

"I don't think peoples' lives are ruined if they still have one to live."

Tim wasn't sure what to say so they watched the rain fall in the beam of the streetlight. Tim started to shiver.

"Come on." Abbey led Tim by the hand to his couch and pulled a blanket over them. They cuddled briefly before Abbey announced, "It smells like David."

They sniffed the fleece that David had used during his nap. It smelled faintly of apple shampoo and Old Spice deodorant.

"Okay, this is like having David sitting here watching us," Abbey said, annoyed as she threw the blanket off. "You're just going to have to put some clothes on if you're cold, mister!"

Tim saw the white flash of her teeth as she grinned in the dark.

"I got another one," he said, pulling an afghan out from behind the couch. "Did they call David about his paper route?"

"He starts Monday."

"He's a really great kid!" Tim said, with the maudlin senti-mentality of a drunk.

"Yeah."

"But when he tells me about something he saw, no matter how I try to shake it, I can't help but feel freaked out."

"I know what you mean."

"You know… I keep writing it off as a hallucination, but one night I saw a woman walk into my bedroom here and she looked just like you, but pregnant."

"Like a ghost?" Abbey asked.

Tim nodded.

"What did she look like?"

CHAPTER 15

The next morning Abbey had the day off. Tim went to her home and they sifted through an old printer box filled with photos.

"I've wanted to scan them and put them in an album," Abbey told him. "I've just been too busy."

There were baby pictures of Abbey and pictures of David. They both looked shabbily dressed in all of them, and none of the photos were professionally taken except for one of Abbey in her track uniform.

"The coach that year handed that to me after practice and said that they were just 'proofs,' but I knew she had paid for them since I couldn't."

"You were disturbingly skinny," Tim said, staring at the tiny girl doing her best to smile at the camera.

Abbey nodded. "There wasn't much to eat."

Tim's heart sank. He wished he could go back in time and rescue the skinny kid in the jersey from what she'd grown up with.

An old print slid out from beneath a stack of other photos and the girl of Tim's nightmares grimaced up at him. She was a close call for Abbey and a dead ringer for the apparition who had invaded his bedroom.

He felt his pulse quicken. "That's her!"

"Aunt J?" Abbey asked in disbelief, picking up the photo.

Tim blanched as if saying the woman's name might conjure her up.

Abbey pursed her lips. "She's the one I told you about who went a little crazy."

The woman in the photo was pretty, like Abbey, but didn't appear as confident and composed as her niece. The left corner of her mouth was drawn up slightly in a coaxed smile as if she wasn't sure what the expression meant. She wore a deplorable red and green Christmas sweater that was too big on her as she stood alone on the front sidewalk of what was now Tim's rental.

"Did she live at my place?" Tim asked fearful of the answer.

"Till I turned five or so. Grandma made her go to the special classes they had for her at the high school. She slept most of the time and kept her door locked a lot."

"I'm sorry, Abbey," Tim offered. "Maybe what I saw wasn't really her."

"I can still remember looking at her 'missing' picture in the grocery store next to that machine you put the quarters in for gumballs and stickers. Grandma offered two thousand dollars if anyone could find her."

"They never did?"

Abbey shook her head. "One time she got up in the middle of the night and ran down the street in just her panties, with no bra. It was freezing cold and windy. Grandma had to chase her and wrestle her down in the snow to cover her with a towel and her parka. About a week later she tried to stab herself in the belly in the kitchen. I can still remember Grandma telling me to stay back, though I wanted to help clean up the blood. I don't know why I held onto the idea that someone with that many problems might still be out there somewhere."

David pushed through the front door, back from his paper-boy job. "Hey."

"Do you remember Aunt Jenny?" Abbey quizzed, proffering David the photo as he approached.

David stared at the picture. "That's our aunt?" he asked, a stunned expression on his face.

"It was," Abbey answered, evidently surprised by the sudden display of emotion.

The boy's eyes remained fixed on the image.

"What is it?"

"She was the girl at the gun range."

"What?"

"I saw her at the range the night the team went to hunt for Jennifer and then again when Tim and I went. Both times I saw a replay of a bunch of guys with letterman jackets all standing around, pushing her down and laughing."

"Did you see who they were?"

"Not their faces, but it seemed like two different things happened out there, because I also got images of someone else, someone bigger, choking her. She looked even more scared than Cassidy Heintz."

Abbey grimaced as David slid the photo back onto the coffee table and examined the other pictures of his relatives.

"Who's that guy?" he asked, pointing to a picture of a jock with a glam-rock haircut and buck teeth glibly looking back at them. He wore a letterman's jacket with a double zero on the shoulder.

"He was some distant cousin that got kicked out of his house and slept at ours for a while," Abbey explained. "Grandma ran him off. It wasn't until later I realized that something weird had started between Aunt J and him. Aunt J even kept that picture on her bedroom wall for a while."

"That's Double-o-mullet!" David said with more certainty than Tim had ever heard in his voice before.

"Doublewho?"

"One of the guys I saw hurting Jennifer had a letterman's jacket with a zero-zero on it. His hair was all feathery, just like that guy. That was as much as I could see. People kept laughing and slapping him on the back, then he'd call her names—stuff like 'retard' and 'slut'—and push her down and they'd all laugh."

***

Tim showered and bicycled over to the school with his classroom keys dangling from a lanyard. The front doors of the building were open. Teams of janitors had rolled up the rugs against the walls as they shampooed the carpeted hallways giving off the scent of something flowery, yet industrial. Tim enjoyed the cool darkness as he approached the big wooden door of the library. Peering at his keys in the dark he jabbed the first one into the lock. It slid in stubbornly. The teeth seeming to catch every angry little pin on the way. As the tumbler clicked and turned a hand landed on Tim's shoulder. Without thinking, Tim took the offending hand in a vice-like grip and bent it backward, doubling his assailant over. Al Buoncuore's usually mischievous face grimaced up at him.

"What are you doing?" the big athletics director groaned in surprise.

Tim didn't know. He still had his hand clamped on the man's wrist, keeping him under submission. He let go and his victim jerked his freed hand back, massaging his wrist, teeth bared in pain.

"I'm sorry," Tim muttered, without really meaning it. He hated being approached from behind.

Buoncuore glared at Tim and carried on rubbing his wrist.

"I'm sorry. I'm just jumpy about my six –my back," Tim clarified.

"I guess!" Al exclaimed, the anger apparent in his voice.

Buoncuore was a big man and a little glimmer of pride came over Tim at having been able to slap a leverage on him so quickly and make him bend.

"I needed to let you know that the league is okay with a cross-country team, if you can find at least three boys who want to run."

"That'd be great," Tim said as if nothing could be more natural after what happened.

"Where'd you learn that stuff?" Al asked, rotating his wrist and frowning. "Army?"

"A friend," Tim said. *Sergeant First Class Alonzo Denny.*

Buoncuore regarded Tim with suspicion. The kind of look that said someone wasn't sure if you belonged in their world.

"Anyway," Buoncuore said, shaking off the pain and putting his hands on his hips, "try not to beat the kids, okay?"

Tim nodded.

"Unless of course they have it coming." Buoncuore laughed before attempting to resume his normal strut-walk down the hallway.

As Tim watched the dark form recede along the row of lockers he felt the familiar nervous stir of adrenaline. *In through the nose out through the mouth.* He repeated the mantra in his head a few times, thankful to be in the cool darkness of the vacant school. Then he went into the library, hoping to be normal again. He thought about turning on the lights, but decided he liked the dark better.

Ironically for an English major, Tim had never really figured out the Dewey decimal system. With the computers unplugged and covered with dust jackets in the darkness he knew the card catalog would be his only option. Luckily, however, when he approached the aged wooden drawers where the tiny index cards were he found the school's collection of yearbooks sitting right there, between two bookends.

Meadowlark High School was small enough that the volumes were relatively thin. They ran all the way from 1938 up to the year before he had started teaching there. Apparently the volume for the most recent year hadn't been added yet.

Abbey had said that their cousin had been kicked out of their home when she was three or four, so he figured he wanted the late 1980s—assuming the kid had even made it into a yearbook at all.

"Wish she had remembered his name," Tim murmured to himself as he ran his finger down the rows of yearbook spines. He pulled the years 1986 to 1988 out and carried them over to the built-in benches by the window.

He placed the picture of the mulleted creep he'd brought with him on the window sill and sat cross-legged with the yearbooks resting in his lap. He wondered if he found a picture of the kid when he was younger if he would recognize him.

The first two yearbooks yielded nothing. He rose and started to go through all of the 1980s, grasping at any potential familiarity.

Midway through 1985, a figure appeared in the doorway of the library.

"Hello, Tim."

Tim peered through the darkness and spotted Eldon Carson, his wranglers looking as creased and pressed as when they had been purchased during the Carter administration. However, today his boots were gone, replaced by a pair of gleaming white New Balance sneakers.

"What's with the shoes, Mr. Carson?" Tim asked, setting the yearbook down and approaching his friend. Privately, he hoped the old man wouldn't ask what he was up to with the yearbooks in the darkened library.

"My granddaughter bought them for me. She's a podiatrist in Salt Lake. I don't like the way they look much, but they do help my arthritis when it's hot like this."

"Arthritis?" Tim asked. Normally, asking an old person about their ailments could be a death sentence, but Carson was a tough old bird.

"Most people get it in the winter, but I'm a true Wyomingite. It's the heat that gets me. So you're going to stick around one more year?"

"Yeah," Tim replied. "I'm looking forward to starting again."

"That's real fine," Carson said, radiating content. "I saw you out with Abbey Jenkins the other day, walking a giant dog."

Small towns suck, Tim thought, even if those who took an interest in your business were as good-natured as Carson.

"Yeah, I just got it from the pound," he responded, trying to divert Carson from his real point of interest.

Carson laughed, knowing full well what Tim was trying to do. His old gray eyes shimmered in the darkness.

"Tell her Mr. Carson is still proud of her," he said. "That little girl was born in hell, but even as a kid you could tell she was clawing her way out. Everyone should be proud of people like her."

Tim nodded. *What could you say to that?*

"It's good that her brother can have a straight-shooting guy around for him to learn from. I got your message, by the way. I'll be happy to talk with him."

"Thanks," Tim said. "He really is a good kid."

"Yes, he is." The old man nodded pensively. "It's horrible that he had to find that little girl. Is he doing okay?"

The question jarred Tim. He had never thought to really ask David if he was all right after what happened. David was just David. He probably saw a lot worse in their shared nightmares.

"I'll tell him that you want to talk with him. He's working on being a cross-country runner."

"I've been meaning to ask you every time I see you, but then I forget—when are you going to join the VFW?" the old man asked.

Tim had absolutely no interest in swapping blood-and-guts stories with the beer-swilling old men of the Veterans of Foreign Wars.

"When we win our war," Tim said, trying to appear nonchalant.

"We need more young-blooded folks in there. I've heard all the old farts tell the same stupid stories over and over again and each time they become a little more heroic and little more unbelievable than the last."

"That's kind of what I was hoping to avoid, Mr. Carson," Tim said with a pained grin, hoping not to hurt the old man's feelings.

"Well, Mr. Ross," Carson said, "could you at least help me move some tables into the VF-dub hall?"

"If that will save me from having to go to their meetings."

"Good man," Carson said, slapping him on the back. "I have my truck. You can ride with me."

They went out to the parking lot, where the old man fired up his ancient green Sierra, which had been built around the time of Tim's birth. It sounded like a dragster, with a slipping serpentine belt that hissed and squealed in and out of place. At some special point known only to Carson, he pulled down on the shifter and the old rattling beast began to roll forward through the empty parking space in front of it.

The VFW hall was only a few miles away. Tim thought he'd humor the old man by riding with him instead of taking his bike.

"The football team helped me load 'em, but now they've all gone home," Carson explained, pointing back at the tables in the back of the truck.

"We'll get 'em," Tim said.

At the Quonset hut that housed the VFW, Tim pulled the tables out of the back of the truck and, though they were unwieldy and long, they weren't heavy. Carson hurried ahead of him and opened the doors.

Inside an assortment of folding chairs on bare concrete rested below a podium near a gas-fired furnace in the corner. An American flag and a VFW flag where posted on either side of a podium at the front of the room. The walls were decked with countless photos, the bigger ones revealing young men staring out from the walls in a variety of sailor suits and khaki uniforms. Some of them had never returned to the Cowboy State. There was also an assortment of Japanese flags and other paraphernalia from wars that were now slowly fading from public memory.

"If you do change your mind, you'd be welcome to come tonight. We're having roast beef."

Tim lugged a table into position and set it up grateful there were only four more.

"You could even bring Abbey."

"I'll think about it," Tim lied good-naturedly as he walked out for more tables.

In five minutes he had all the tables set up according to the old man's specifications and then the two began to push the worn folding chairs along the concrete to the tables.

"The ladies' auxiliary will come by later with tablecloths," Carson said, biting his lip thoughtfully as he plotted the best arrangement for a roast beef dinner.

"Where's yours?" Tim asked, gesturing towards the walls of military photos, anxious to offer the old man a conciliatory gesture since he didn't want to go to the dinner.

"I was in the Tenth Mountain," Carson said, hurrying to the wall and pointing to a young, confident man with skis who looked only a little like him. Then he pointed to the far wall, by the doorway. "You would be our first soldier who fought in the Iraq War," he added, as if this should change Tim's mind for him. "We have two sailors and a Marine from your generation, but you'd be the first army."

Tim walked over to Carson and looked at the pictures of the sailors and a female Marine. Next to the fledgling display of Iraq war veterans was one for the War in the Persian Gulf. Tim gazed in envy at the desert camo-clad troops who stared back at him.

You were lucky. A forty-seven day war...

He became aware of a familiar pair of eyes looking back at him from the photograph. He was thinner and he had traded in his mullet for a shorn head, but it was definitely Abbey's wayward cousin staring back at Tim with his buck teeth and the same stupid grin. The label below read PFC Brinker, Adam.

"Did you know this kid?" Tim said a little more urgently than he would have liked.

Carson moved from his own photo to that of the private and squinted at it, then frowned. "His name was something Brinker. I remember he was a cocky little punk when he first came back. Spending his money at the bars and getting drunk and fighting. He bought a big motorcycle and rode it around all the time, trying to fit in with the local trash." The old man shook his head. "They arrested him in Evanston for nearly stabbing a girl to death. I remember his idiot lawyer got him committed to the state home there by saying he was a vet and had had a hard time and all that. Tell me, Tim, did you enjoy your war?"

Tim didn't reply.

"Did you like what you saw there? What we did?"

Tim shook his head, almost willing to tell the old man just how bad it had really been.

"I loved being up in those mountains," Carson went on, pointing back at his own picture, "but I never liked the reason we were there. I don't know of anyone that loved war—at least, not the ones who were really in one…" He shook his head again. "Never in my life would I run around pulling that crap, acting like a parasite." He turned to Tim. "That's why we need men like you here." He clapped Tim on the shoulder. "Men who do what they have to and then come home and find a job and a girl."

Tim nodded hollowly. He didn't want to be here anymore. He didn't want to hear it anymore. He was one of the damaged, one of the wounded, and Carson's admiration only showed how naïve he could be.

He let Carson thank him and then ran to the school to pick up his bike, politely declining the old man's repeated offer to give him a ride.

CHAPTER 16

Tim phoned The State Home in Evanston and to his surprise found that they still had one Brinker, Adam in residence. The nasal-sounding woman on the line insisted that to meet with a patient Tim had to be family and that minors, even if they were family, needed to be accompanied by an adult at all times. Tim caught up with Abbey before she left for work. David was out on his paper route.

"You'll be right there with him?" Abbey asked uncertainly as she picked at her scrambled eggs.

"For sure! I wouldn't leave him alone in there."

Abbey didn't seem reassured.

"I know it's not ideal, but I'm not sure how else to find out what really happened."

"What about telling the police—you know, like they asked us to do?" Abbey suggested.

"If you had done something terrible to someone how bad would you want to tell the police? I don't think they'd be allowed to interrogate a mental patient, at least not in any useful way."

"So *you're* going to beat him into a confession while my little brother watches?" said Abbey, frowning and pushing her plate away.

"I think talking to this guy under the guise of David just wanting to get to know his cousin better might be the best way to find out more. We'll see what he says about growing up here, ask about the other relatives… you know."

"You think he'll just randomly bring up, 'Oh yeah, when I wasn't playing football or working on cars as a teenager back in Meadowlark, sometimes I also enjoyed an incestuous relationship with my cousin who I murdered, or at least assaulted at the gun range?'"

"If he's crazy enough, maybe!" Tim offered the toothy grin of a salesman, hoping to win Abbey over to his side or at least get a smile out of her. "I'm just trying to help."

Abbey rose from the table and scraped her breakfast into the trash. "You should have been a detective," she muttered.

"So... is it cool?"

"Just don't leave David alone in there, okay?"

"I wouldn't dream of it."

Tim rose to embrace her as she left for work. Though they kissed, he could tell she wasn't happy.

***

The receptionist called Tim back a little before noon and said that Brinker had agreed to accept a visit from David. Tim doubted he had any idea who the boy was, but imagined after being locked up in Crazyville for so many years he would probably accept a visit from anyone. Tim thought he might hear a list of things they weren't supposed to bring, like metal objects, and all kinds of protocols, but all Nasal said was, "bring a photo ID for both of you."

Tim made sure David had his student ID in the old canvas and Velcro wallet he carried and the pair set out over the sagebrush flats in Tim's Subaru.

Tim should have been more excited to be on the road, like a bloodhound on a trail, but unnerving Abbey that morning bothered him more than upsetting any other girl he had dated before.

"You ever been on a road trip?" he asked David, hoping to distract himself as he signaled and then exited at the Flying J

Truck stop just out of town.

"We went to Lagoon one time with school," the boy answered, meaning the old amusement park north of Salt Lake City two hours away.

"Anywhere else?" Tim asked as they got out of the car and headed towards the fluorescent-lit mecca of hydrogenated oils and high fructose corn syrup.

The boy shook his head.

"Never even Yellowstone or the Red Desert?" Tim said incredulously.

"No."

"Before school starts, I'm taking you and Abbey on some trips," Tim promised as the sliding doors rolled open before them and they went inside.

"Abbey wants to. She's just too poor and too busy."

"I'll take care of it," Tim said as they ran their eyes over the coolers of chocolate milk and energy drinks. "Anyway, the best thing about being on the road is all the crap you get to eat, so pick whatever you want and I'll pay for it."

Tim chose a bratwurst, a chocolate milk and a bag of M&Ms. After an unnecessary amount of label studying the boy picked a bottle of water and a small bag of lightly salted peanuts.

"Here, try these," Tim said, thrusting a big box of Twinkies into the boy's chest and forcing him to wrap his gangly arms around them as they made their way to the register.

Back in the car, Tim had eaten almost all the Twinkies he had forced on the boy by the time the I-80 dived off a summit onto barren plains of sagebrush and rock that seemed to stretch out forever west.

"Will he be tied up?" David asked suddenly. "Like Hannibal Lecter?"

"I don't think so," Tim said, having pictured the encounter

being something more like a routine prison visit, with jump-suits and metal detectors. "At least, not if they're letting him see people. I got yer back though."

Just get through this—talk to the guy, find out he had nothing to do with it, and make sure David talks to Carson so we can all get back on track.

Tim signaled to pass a semi climbing the last hill before Evanston.

"Can we go to Eugene?" David asked.

"Where?"

"Eugene, Oregon," David said, watching the landscape blur past the windows. "It's where the Nike Museum is."

Tim tried not to laugh. "Yeah," he agreed, "if that's where you'd like to go. It's better than some of the places we've gone so far. While we're there we could go up to Astoria and have our pictures taken in front of the Goonies House."

"What's the goonies house?"

"You know *The Goonies!*" Tim said.

There was no recognition in the boy's eyes.

Tim shook his head in disbelief. "Anyway, we'll watch *The Goonies* tonight and get our pictures taken when we go to Oregon."

The pair took the first Evanston exit and drove into the grounds of the Wyoming State Hospital. Red-brick buildings overlooked well-kept lawns, making it look like a small private school. A group of fat, sedate-looking men wearing vinyl ID tags on their collars smoked on the sidewalk just outside the main entrance.

After presenting their own IDs to a chubby woman in scrubs at the front desk, Tim and David were led to a small room where they sat on plastic chairs at a wooden table.

Tim had expected a scene from *One Flew Over the Cuckoo's*

Nest. Big mean-looking guys in white coats. Bars on the windows. People screaming as they were wrestled into straitjackets. Instead, the whole place resonated with a quiet peacefulness that made Tim suspicious.

Tim fingered his plastic 'VISITOR' tag awkwardly until the far door opened and a small blond-haired man walked in. Roughly twenty years had passed since the service photo at the VFW had been taken at the Marine Corps Recruit Depot in San Diego. The mullet and the Marine Corps haircut had now been replaced by a boring civilian cut parted from the left side. The cocky expression he had worn with his letterman's jacket had softened into a welcoming expression of calm.

"Hello," he said politely, revealing the buck teeth Tim remembered from the photo.

Tim made it a point to stand up and study the man carefully. He didn't stand up out of respect or to shake Brinker's hand. He did it to show Brinker that he was bigger than him.

"Hello. This is your cousin David," he said, leaving out the boy's last name intentionally as if it were some protection. "He wanted to meet you." He sat down again, stiffly, keeping his back ramrod-straight and his eyes focused on Brinker.

"Hello," Brinker said to David. "I'm Adam."

He reached out and shook the boy's hand, a gesture Tim watched carefully. Then Brinker took a seat across from them, leaned back in his chair, and rested his left ankle on his right knee. Tim glimpsed some sort of little plastic box strapped to his leg, something like what people on house arrest wore.

Tim was surprised how relaxed Brinker was. It wasn't the artificial cool of someone being cocky or rude. He was the calmest person in the room.

"I'm glad you came to meet me," Brinker said, smiling as warmly as an aged clergyman on Easter Sunday reunited with one of his flock.

"Are we really cousins?" David asked.

"That's what they tell me. I do sort of remember your sister when I lived in the white house back there in Meadowlark, but I don't remember you."

"How long did you live there?" Tim interrupted.

Brinker turned from the boy and smiled at Tim. "I don't remember real well. Are you a cousin, too?" he asked, not with any sense of malice as if he liked the idea of an unexpected reunion.

"I'm..." Tim hesitated, not having thought of a good cover. "I'm dating his sister," Tim told him, cocking his head at the boy.

"So you'll be family soon," Brinker said, smiling as if this was the best news he had heard for a while.

Tim raised his eyebrows, not knowing what to say, but realized that getting Brinker to talk might be harder than he'd thought.

"What do you like to do?" Brinker asked David.

David thought about it for a moment. "I like to run a lot."

"That's great!" Brinker said, his voice suddenly a little too loud for the confined space. "You gotta stay fit!"

"You run a lot in the Marine Corps?" Tim asked.

Brinker tossed his head back and spread his arms out as if on a crucifix and laughed. "Oh man, did I ever!"

Tim was reminded of a kid's TV show host, the sort who would soon be found to have a collection of human skulls in the basement.

"You kill anybody while you were in?" Tim asked as if they might share a special bond.

Brinker didn't respond, but Tim could see his jaw go taut beneath his skin. David shot Tim a nervous look, but Tim ignored it.

Brinker let the lip on the back of his chair grind over his back before he rocked forward onto fists that knuckled into the table, elbows bent, body canted toward Tim and David. His thumb gave a slight twitch and his eyes seemed to dance with something awful and remembered. His buck toothed smile did not go above the top row of his glistening white teeth.

"You've been there, haven't you?" he said, staring at Tim with narrowed eyes. "You've killed yourself a raghead or two as well, haven't you?"

As soon as Brinker had said it, Tim's shield failed briefly for a moment as the woman who had been in his sights suddenly flashed in his mind. The man across the table caught Tim's change in expression and his nasty smile traveled up to his eyes.

"Yeah, I thought so. Nobody can have that creepy look if he hasn't looked death in the face and rubbed sweaty thighs with him."

"So did *you* kill anybody?" Tim repeated, trying to turn the focus of the conversation back onto Brinker.

"You tell me if you think I did," Brinker said, his eyes dancing. The mean, toothy grin spread from ear to ear.

Tim glared at those buck teeth for a moment before replying, "I think you played with yourself and annoyed the piss out of the women reporters, who you stared at all day but were too scared to talk to, until your NCO told you to stay away from them."

Brinker slapped the table with an open hand, making a loud thunk that reverberated through the room.

"I'll tell you if you tell me," he said.

Tim felt David's eyes on him as he waited for a response. He hesitated and wished the boy wasn't there, but then he nodded.

Brinker leaned back in his chair, beaming at the private

victory he had just won. "Did you cut 'em up?"

Tim frowned, hearing the crack of his rifle and seeing the burqa woman going limp, flopping like a sack of dirty laundry on the baked earth.

Brinker stared at Tim with a rumpled expression fit for Jack Nicholson in the Overlook Hotel. "I tell you, killer, when we chased 'em out of Kuwait City they were all along the side of the road, toasted to a crisp in their own nasty grease. Like they'd been dipped in Pennzoil and then deep fried by Satan himself!"

Tim ran his tongue along his teeth, remembering well the images of the charred corpses he had seen in documentaries about The First Gulf War.

Brinker's mouth went slack and he appeared to listen to something far away. Then his eyes grew fierce. "Can you believe it that when I cut off one's ear to take home they hit me with UCMJ?"

"What's UCMJ?" David asked.

"Military law," Tim murmured.

"It's a bunch of politics and garbage is what it is!"

Frustrated and afraid for David, Tim pulled a color photocopy of Aunt Jenny from the lowest pocket of his cargo shorts and slid it across the table. "Have you ever seen this girl?"

Brinker looked down at the picture and then up at his visitors. "Who are you?"

"David's your cousin and I'm his sister's boyfriend."

"Are you feds?"

Tim shook his head. "Why would we be feds?"

"I'm not saying anything," Brinker said, sliding the picture back at them.

"Did you hurt her?" Tim asked.

Brinker shook his head. "It wasn't me."

"Someone did hurt her, then?" Tim asked.

"I'm not talking to you."

"You know what happened to that girl," Tim said, not really knowing for sure, but giving it a shot. "You tell me who hurt her and I go away," he promised. "I didn't hear it from you—I don't know who told me. I'll never come back here."

"I didn't cut her!" Brinker yelled.

"I don't think you did," Tim said, glancing at David watching the exchange with more interest than he usually showed towards anything. "I think someone strangled her."

The crazed patient opposite them shook his head vigorously and shot a glance at the door. "I wasn't there!"

"You weren't where?"

Brinker eyed Tim cautiously. He gave another desperate look at the door and then leaned forward. "It was Trent that really hurt her."

"Trent who?"

"Trent Mortensen," Brinker hissed.

"Trent Mortensen?"

"Yeah, Trent and some of the other guys from the football team. They went out to the range, wanted to get her drunk and..."

"Don't lie to me!" Tim growled, not wanting to attract anyone's attention in the hall just off the room.

"I really didn't hurt her that bad. I tell her when I see her sometimes that I woulda stopped 'em if I'd had known how."

"You see her?" David interrupted.

The man nodded and his gaze slipped to the empty seat next to him as if she were there.

"Is she here now?" Tim asked skeptically.

"What do you think?"

"I'm asking you."

Brinker frowned down at his watch and shook his head. "Not right now, but I do see her sometimes. Still wearing those Christmas sweaters."

"Let's get out of here," Tim said to David, ignoring the forlorn figure before them.

They left the ward quickly, relieved to be out of there before anyone questioned their interrogation of a patient.

***

The sun was disappearing below the horizon in the rearview mirror on the drive back to Meadowlark. Its last intense rays of light gave the sagebrush a yellow glow at its edges.

"You killed people?" David asked.

Tim watched a cardboard box skitter over the road in the wind before responding. "Yeah."

"What was it like?"

"It was bad, David."

"How many?"

Tim hesitated, imagining the people. He'd made their insides spray red or pink, had watched them fall in the dirt or onto the concrete. He'd continued to fire at one who limped away to better cover. He'd stared at the dirty blood of the one he'd shot in that windowsill.

"I don't know," he said, honestly, and shaking his head. "I try not to count. I think six."

"Wow!"

"I haven't told anyone that but you."

"Why do you feel bad about it, if that's what you are supposed to do?"

Tim shrugged. "I guess 'cause none of the people that say you're supposed to do it, none of the politicians or patriotic blowhards are the ones who pull the trigger. The worst part is, when it's over you wonder if you really needed to do it, or if doing it really made anything better."

"What do you mean?"

"Nothing they taught us in boot camp or anywhere else really accounted for how messy things really were. How people look when you shoot them, how your friends still die even after you start killing the people killing them. How eventually you'll just sort of shut yourself off so that you don't have to think too hard about it. Then, when you come home, you sort of shut yourself off from everyone else because you feel like you don't deserve to have what you took away from the people you killed."

"Did you shut yourself off from me?"

Tim looked at the kid in surprise and then back at the yellow line. "Yeah. I'm sorry. I should have known about your mom dying. You were in my class all year and even in a small town like this I had no idea. I should have tried to help."

David shrugged. "I'm doing okay."

"I should have tried to help Heather Brady, too, but I was just... aloof."

"What would it take for you to stop being *aloof*?"

"I dunno."

A cicada flew up and exploded yellow-green on the windshield.

"Is this why you're trying to find out what happened with my family? To make something right?"

Tim wanted to blow the kid off, but he couldn't. "I guess that's part of it, yeah."

David paused. They were nearing the exit for Meadowlark. "That guy we talked to?"

"Uh-huh?"

"He had a woman in middle-eastern clothes, like the ones on TV, standing next to him, glaring. Her ears were cut off."

CHAPTER 17

That night Tim, Abbey and David watched *The Goonies* while eating burgers they'd brought home from Chuck's. After the movie, David played on his computer and Tim told Abbey about what had happened in Evanston, wondering how mad she might be after he told her what had happened.

"So he's officially one of us," she said, frowning.

"What?"

"He met one of our crazy relatives and had a crazy-ish experience with him. I guess it was bound to happen."

"I'm sorry," Tim said. "I didn't know Brinker would react like that. I just wanted to help you find out what had really happened."

"I know." She gave a sad smile. "Don't beat yourself up again, okay? I didn't mean to be weird this morning either. I just… worry about both of you."

"Me?" Tim laughed. "There's nothing to worry about with me. I could disappear tomorrow and the world would be better off."

"Tim!" she snapped. "Don't say that!"

She reached across the table and took both of his hands. He could feel the surprising warmth of her palms spreading into his own.

"I don't want anything to ever happen to you," she said earnestly. "So don't talk that way."

Tim felt the defensive grin he wanted to flash fail to appear. "Okay."

She held him in her gaze for a while longer before releasing him and going to the fridge. "So did you do anything else on your trip to the crazy house? Go see the buffalo at the park?"

She produced a gallon of water and brought it to the table with two glasses.

"We went to the Flying J for snacks and on the way over David said he wanted to go to the Nike factory in Oregon."

She laughed. "Does he think they'll give him a free pair of shoes or something?"

Tim shrugged.

"He doesn't ask for much," she confided. "I'd be happy to do it if I could afford it."

"What if we all went? Don't worry about the money," Tim said.

"You sure?"

"Of course," he said, only hesitating for a moment before adding, "it'd be the best thing I've done in forever."

Abbey shot a surreptitious glance at David to check that he was still distracted by his computer then leaned in and kissed Tim.

After returning to his own house that night, Tim pulled out the phone book that had come with the rental. Only slightly thinner than a teen novel, the phone book showed Trent Mortensen living at 5544 County Road 12.

***

County Road 12 was like all the other oil and gravel roads stretching through the countryside. Lined by cottonwoods, irrigation ditches and barbed wire fences, this morning it almost turned gold in the early sun. Rolling over the culverts that spanned Muddy Creek, Tim spotted a rusting yellow crane stretching its arm above the cattails in the ditch bank and holding up the sign he had been looking for.

Mortensen Service—Towing, Wrecking & Repairs

A junkyard of old cars and machinery stretched out over what passed for someone's front yard on the left side of the road. Tim signaled, even though he was the only person on the road, and drove over the cattle guard onto the Mortensen spread. A rusty swing set with faded yellow candy stripes stood amid the refuse in front of an old tin trailer. The salty stench of oil and two barking dogs greeted Tim as he pulled in.

A shirtless little boy with wild, long curly hair and a torso tanned to leather rode an old pink bicycle around Tim's car. Tim studied the scene for a moment. Blue light flashed from the open door of a Quonset hut and he decided he might forgo a stop at the trailer and a lot of difficult questions from a wife or girlfriend and try the hut first.

Upon opening the car door, one of the dogs rushed to sniff his leg and inspect him before he could even get out. It responded well to a pat on the head and a rubbing of the ears. The other one, a big pit-rottweiler mix, stood a few yards off. Its muscles and testicles bulged under its skin and it bared its teeth as Tim closed the car door. He looked for the boy to call it off, but the child had fled, leaving his empty bike on its side in front of the shop.

Tim crouched and scooped up a handful of the biggest stones from the dirt drive. The dog suddenly dipped its head and followed him with weary eyes. Many of the dogs Tim had seen in Iraq were like this—mean, dump-hound scavengers, more wolves or dingoes than man's best friend.

What kind of people only have mean dogs? It was something he had often asked himself in Iraq.

Tim walked towards the shop, shaking his hand to make the stones clack together in his palm and keeping the angry mutt in the corner of his left eye. The dog circled behind him as he walked towards the Quonset hut, cutting him off from his car.

When he reached the doorway of the shop Tim flicked the stones backward, not looking behind but hoping to hear a "yipe," but if they did nail the dog he didn't hear anything.

The flashing sparks of acetylene cast the shadows of unidentifiable machinery onto the walls as Tim set foot on the oily concrete of the shop. An assemblage of equipment from vices to grinders and pounders flanked a 1950s Buick and a 1980s Toyota Celica. Both looked like hopeless patients in the worst wing of an automobile hospital. Hammers and wrenches hung on the walls amid faded centerfolds with feathered 1980s haircuts. A very poorly stuffed antelope head missing an eye loomed over an old radio that blared the awful twang of a country music station.

The boy who had greeted Tim on his arrival was nowhere to be seen, but a fat man with a welder's mask and coveralls busied himself with a welding torch on the body of a Kubota tractor. He didn't seem to be aware that he had company. As Tim approached he looked apprehensively at the sparks flying in all directions and opted to keep his distance. He picked up a hubcap from the floor and twanged it against a steel girder.

The welder stopped and raised his mask to study Tim, revealing a man in his forties with a big nose and white beard, his dirty face already starting to show its age.

"You Trent Mortensen?" Tim asked.

The welder squinted as if he didn't understand the question, then hurried across the shop and killed the radio.

"What?" he called like a deaf man.

"I'm looking for Trent Mortensen," Tim said, raising his voice.

"What can I do for you?" the welder asked amicably.

Tim pulled the picture of Aunt Jenny from his cargo shorts and showed it to the man. "You seen her before?"

Mortensen approached, reaching out a gloved hand and took

the photo to study it. "No."

"You sure?" Tim asked.

"I'm sure!" he said, nodding.

"Didn't you go to high school here?"

"Who are you?" Mortensen asked, staring at Tim with eyes that were growing more intense.

"I'm a friend of her family," Tim said. "You don't remember seeing a crazy-looking girl wearing Christmas sweaters all months of the year when you were growing up here?"

The man turned and shook his head as he walked back to the tractor and flipped his welding mask down over his face.

"You don't remember her name?" Tim persisted. "Never saw her around?"

The man ignored him as he fired the torch and its blue flame kissed the welding rod as he tried to remarry parts of the tractor back together.

Tim hadn't anticipated this. Most of all he regretted how the welder's mask hid Mortensen's expression.

He moved in closer.

"Yesterday I talked to Adam Brinker. He's a weird, crazy guy, in the State Home over in Evanston. The one lucid thing that he said was how you and he and some of the lettermen took Jennifer Jenkins out to the gun range and, well…"

Tim let the sentence trail off, but in doing so made the mistake of taking his eyes off his quarry. The next thing he knew three hundred and fifty pounds of Trent Mortensen came barreling towards him. The man flipped off his welder's mask and pushed his bulbous nose right into Tim's face.

"I don't know what you're talking about!" He spat, his breath stale and hot. "I didn't know that girl. I don't know any Brinker. I stopped drinking and became a Christian in June of ninety-eight and if you don't get out of here right now I'm going to cross back over."

Tim grinned at the red-faced, big-nosed man. He couldn't help himself—not because he thought even on the best of days he could take the big man, but because long ago he'd grown tired of the whole world trying to scare him. He had seen too much and had decided at some point that at least he would not show anyone that he was afraid.

"Mr. Mortensen," Tim said, his voice calm, "two of my friends lost one of the few connections they had to family in that girl."

The big man's eyes bulged angry and afraid.

"I'm not a cop. I don't want trouble. I just want to know what happened to her so they can put it behind them. They just want to know what happened and where her body is."

"Body?" The man said, leaning back a little and screwing up his nose in genuine confusion.

"What happened to her after she died?"

"She's dead?"

"*Someone* killed her out there," Tim insisted.

Mortensen shook his head. "I'm not the same person I used to be. I was a stupid drunk kid who didn't ever think about anyone else, but I never killed nobody!"

"You think maybe the other guys did?"

"I don't know, but if they did it wasn't when I was there. First day of school after it happened, her grandma drives into the high school parking lot with her in the passenger seat and the girl points us out. Gramma slams on the brakes and rushes out of the car and points a double-barrel shotgun in my face. Tells me if I ever talk to that girl again, she'll blow my head off."

Tim wanted to smile, but didn't want to interrupt Mortensen in his sudden desire to come clean.

"I stayed completely away from her after that, but I remember that girl used to catch up with me and tell me that she had a boyfriend now and he was going to kill me and my friends."

"You ever see this boyfriend?"

"No. I think she was lying, but I was done with her after that grandma of hers. I think most of those other guys were, too, 'cause they didn't want no twelve gauges in their faces neither."

"Thank you for your time," Tim said as he turned and walked away wondering what kind of assault charges might be pressed against the big man if anyone came forward, or if they were even within the statute of limitations.

"Mister!" the welder shouted after Tim as he neared the exit, "I'm sorry for getting riled up. I'm not the same person I used to be, but it's hard to change—and it's even harder when people bring up who you were before."

Tim turned and noted the conviction in Mortensen's expression.

"Please tell the family I'm sorry and that I never bothered her again."

Tim nodded and walked to his car, keeping a cautious eye out for the dog. As he drove to Abbey's house he brushed aside the feeling that he had failed and wondered if he could surprise his girlfriend with dinner before she came home. But then that, too, went out of his head. A Meadowlark police Bronco rested in David's driveway and Officer Farner stood with David on the rickety steps of the trailer.

CHAPTER 18

Tim bolted out of his car and up to the porch.

"You okay, Dave?" he blurted out.

David nodded.

"Where's Abbey?"

"At work."

"Mr. Ross," Farner said, reaching to shake Tim's hand, "we want to see if David would be willing to help us with some police work."

Tim shrugged, feeling his pulse slow as he leaned cautiously against the banister. "You'll have to ask Abbey."

"Yeah, we visited her at the vet clinic today and she said it would be all right as long as you were with him when we went."

Tim frowned.

"Basically, we'd go to some of the sites where bodies have been found and other areas we think might be a place to leave a body and see if David can get…" The deputy struggled for the right word, "…impressions, or anything."

"What do you think?" Tim asked David.

David shrugged.

"Are you fine with it?"

"I can't tell when there's a body buried somewhere just by being there," David responded. "Like, if I go to the cemetery I don't see visions or anything."

"Would you be willing to go out on a limb for us?" Farner asked. "Something told you where Cassidy Heintz was."

"If I help you, will you buy me a burger, fries and a medium chocolate and peanut butter milkshake?" the boy asked.

"Sure," Tim said, surprised. "I've never seen you eat that

much before."

"No," David protested, pointing at the policeman, "I want *him* to buy it!"

Farner's eyebrows rose. "Sure," he said, bemused.

"Will you buy me a burger, too?" Tim asked, grinning.

"We'll see," Farner said flatly.

As they left the porch Tim almost made a joke about whether or not the kid would be able to eat all that fast food if they found another corpse, but decided against it. They piled into the police Bronco and, for the second time in a few days, Tim found himself in a cop car. This time he rode in the back seat. Oddly, there were no barriers between the front and the back, probably because it was an older vehicle and the local department didn't arrest that many people.

They started on the main road out of town, but then stopped in front of the library where a light green Toyota Prius sat in a parking spot. Jackson Emmons, reporter extraordinaire for *The Meadowlark Call*, stepped out of the driver seat.

"You comin'?" Farner called.

Emmons nodded and made for the back door of the Bronco.

"Is he writing another story?" Tim asked.

"He wants to do a follow-up story about the search for Cassidy's killer," the cop explained. "You don't mind, do you? Any publicity we can garner to keep the case fresh in the public's mind might lead to tips."

"Hey, Battle," Tim said as the reporter piled into the back seat with a notepad and coffee. "Nice car," he added with a smirk, indicating the Prius.

"You like that?" Emmons asked coldly.

"I guess instead of gender reassignment surgeries for men now they just prescribe a Prius and your ovaries grow right in,"

"Haaaa!" Jackson fake laughed. "Did you know that with every high and tight you get they shave a little off your IQ, too?"

"Mine was better," Tim said.

Jackson nodded. "You're right. I should spend more time on them. It's just that I'm so busy having to work for a living."

"There you go!" Tim said approvingly.

Just out of town Farner signaled and pulled off the blacktop highway onto an oil-slicked road and headed south towards the foreboding peaks of the Uintas.

"We've interviewed the Heintz family, the girl's friends, the camp staff, everyone she knew or who she was friends with, and any weird encounters she'd had lately. We're hoping if David can tell us anything about what he sees or feels or... however he does it when we visit some of these sites, it might give us more information."

Emmons produced a pocket notepad and began to scribble. "David, can you tell me more what it's like when you have one of these visions or impressions you get?"

David did his best to explain and Farner ended up asking the most questions about what started the visions and what David could actually see.

The Bronco climbed above high meadows and pastures, where summer cattle still grazed, and caught up with more cowboys herding their stock across the road.

The deputy smiled and waved. The cattlemen did the same.

"That's my cousin and uncle," he explained after the herd had passed. "They're moving their cows down early. It's been such a hot summer they haven't had anything to graze on up here."

Tim wondered at this, about how so many people in these parts were related. After finding out about the murders it had started him wondering if some type of nepotism could be responsible for letting killings happen in a town where everyone knew everyone else and their business.

They crossed several more cattle guards and the road became rougher and narrower. The shoulder was thick with pine trees that grew arrow straight out of the parched soil. Tim could smell their thick, gluey, Christmas smell wafting through the window, along with the odor of dust. Many of the trees were dead but were still adorned with a plumage of brown pine needles.

"It's been so warm in the winter here lately the bark beetles don't die. So we have that," Farner explained, pointing at the dead branches. "I wonder if we'll have much of a forest left after they're done with it and the fires set in."

He turned right down another narrow two-track road where healthy stands of pine still seemed to be making a go of it as their ragged branches swiped at the sides of the Bronco.

"The first site I want you to see is where Heather Brady's body was found by two hunters." The cop pulled the vehicle onto the side of the two-track road in front of a swift-moving creek. "We'll have to walk a ways," he announced.

They exited the Bronco and started following the water upstream in single file. Their route took them up a sharp incline where the creek tumbled over the rocks. At the top was the meadow and the old cabin Tim had seen from the air and in last spring's headline.

"We believe that the suspect led Brady up here when she was still alive, because the investigators found opened cans of beans and peaches, like someone had been staying here for a while."

Tim frowned at what might have gone on in the dark recesses behind those thick log walls. No glass remained in the windows and the voids seemed like the black eyes of a snake, expressionless and silent about what they'd borne witness to.

"I think you're right," David said, looking at the hovel.

"Why?" Farner asked.

David didn't respond. He set out across the sagebrush towards the shack while the three men followed him. The reporter quickly scribbled something on his little notepad when David stopped at the doorway and peered in for a moment before stepping inside with the others in tow.

Tim was thankful that the cabin was tiny and therefore less menacing than the big old place where they'd found Cassidy Heintz. Stepping inside, he smelled dirt and something like rotting leaves. On the far wall, crosses, rotting stuffed animals, and candles in bottles beaded with wax rested amid wilting plastic flowers. There was no furniture except for some cupboards and a giant cast iron stove no one wanted to lug away in the corner that seemed to serve as a kitchen.

Deputy Farner pointed at the far corner of the cabin, to a hole in the floor littered with memorials and fading mementos. "She was buried where the floorboards had rotted away. She probably wouldn't have been found if one of the hunter's dogs didn't go nuts and start digging there."

Heather Brady stared back from a wreath of red plastic roses at the place where she had been interred. There were a few other pictures of her on the memorial. Some looked like they were copies of the webcam photo once attached to telephone poles or had been taken by a cell phone as she pouted her heavily made-up face and puckered her lips, trying to look sexy. In a big photo the size of a piece of printer paper that someone had placed inside a wreath, she gave a crooked but beautiful, bashful smile. It was the kind of school photo a parent would look at with all the happiness possible, believing that their offspring had an opportunity to do something significant in the world. It made Tim feel terrible that he would have picked the webcam picture as a better representation of the murdered girl's life.

Jackson produced a small camera from his pocket and began to take pictures of the memorial. The camera's flash burst white in the low light of the cabin.

Tim shook his head, feeling angry that so many people had come all the way up here to leave a memento for the girl, but none of them had seemed to care enough to befriend her or look out for her. People just like him.

"I used to come up here and look through the stuff, trying to find out if anyone had said anything in the cards or graffiti that might help us," Farner said, before shooting a sudden look of concern at Jackson. "Don't print that!"

Emmons nodded assuring as he continued taking pictures.

"This is the third time I've been here this year. It looks like the pile has quit growing at least," Farner added.

"She lived here with him for a few days," David said, looking up at the walls. "It was like they were playing house or something."

"Playing house?" the officer asked.

"That's kinda what I get," the boy told him.

The reporter quickly jotted something down and snapped a picture of David.

"Any idea who she was playing house with?"

David shook his head. "Heather is cooking for him and smiling at him and they seem to be happy together, kind of like kids 'playing house.'" David said the phrase oddly, as if he didn't quite understand it. "Like they were play acting at being married and she thought she was going to live here with him. She talks about cleaning the place up and buying a TV."

Tim surveyed the wreckage of the house with disgust.

"You're saying she went here willingly with him?" Farner asked.

David nodded. "Yeah, she really liked him. She keeps smiling and stuff." He closed his eyes and his brow furrowed. "He did kill her here." He shook his head. "I see him move towards her and start to choke her and she looks..." David stopped, looking sick. "She looks... terrible."

"Can you see his face?" Farner asked his voice rising.

David shook his head.

"Are you sure?"

David lurched and his eyes shot wide open. "I've heard this guy before!"

"What?" Tim asked.

The boy shook his head in disbelief. "His voice—I've heard him before!"

"You mean you've heard him say something before?" Farner asked.

"No! I mean I've heard the sound of his voice somewhere before!" David nearly shouted as the journalist scribbled frantically on his notepad.

"Usually I never hear anyone say anything, but here I hear him threatening her or something."

"What exactly is he saying?" Jackson asked.

"The words don't make sense, but I've heard the sound of this guy's voice before!"

"In your visions or..." Farner pried.

"No! I don't know where. It's like hearing the guy from the Motel Six commercials. I recognize the voice!"

The officer continued to probe, asking more questions about the voice and the face, but David ignored him, mouthing something he had heard in the vision to himself, as if trying to call back the sound of the killer's voice.

Eventually, Farner grew discouraged and gave his unlikely posse a ride home. He did, however, insist that David should go with him to another site soon.

CHAPTER 19

David and Tim finished their tenth run since the day Tim had invited the kid for a burger.

"You ready for school?" Tim asked as they neared the boy's trailer.

"Yeah," David said. "I gotta go talk to Jim and Merv about running cross-country, but I think they'll do it. I'll stop and ask on my paper route."

David was at liberty to deliver *The Meadowlark Call* any time before five p.m.—another quirky element of small-town charm. Jim and Merv, the amateur photographers of mutilated cattle, were David's only friends. They lived in a nicer subdivision on the south side of town. They abhorred most sports, natural light, and anything that didn't come from a computer screen. Also, like David, they were tall and skinny so Tim thought they would at least be a start for a cross-country team.

"Good. Tell them practice starts in a week and they need to be there," Tim said as they pulled up to the place where David would split off and go to his house.

"They don't know any girls who might want to run, do they?" Tim asked doubtfully. "Real ones, ones who live on this planet, maybe even ones who live in this town and not in a chat room if we're really lucky."

"I'll see."

"Make sure to hydrate, Dave, you're starting to cottonmouth. When's the deputy going to buy you your cheeseburger?" Tim asked over his shoulder as he turned towards his own house.

"He said after we go on another mission together."

"Don't let him screw you, all right?"

David smiled.

"You going with them today? Do I need to go with you?"

"I kinda don't want to go today."

"Why not?"

"'Cause it's my birthday."

He turned on his heel and quickly caught up with the boy. "What do you want for your birthday?"

"Nothing."

"We gotta do something, man, it's your birthday. I wish I'd known sooner."

"Whatever you want," David said, stopping to face Tim. "I usually go out to lunch with Abbey at twelve thirty-two, because I was born at twelve thirty-two. Even when she was taking summer classes at college she'd come home and take me out to lunch, so I guess she'll do that again."

Tim nodded. "Well, tonight is on me. We'll all go out again and fatten you up and by this afternoon I need to know what you want—a video game, a Tomahawk cruise missile, I dunno… whatever, and we'll go to Evanston and get it."

"Okay," David said. "Maybe we can go shooting again?"

"For sure," Tim said, not sure he ever wanted to return to the gun range with the kid, though he didn't say that. "Happy Birthday!" he shouted before taking off towards his own house.

When Tim arrived home he called Abbey at work and asked what he should buy David for his birthday.

"Birthdays were kind of a disappointment for both of us most of the time as kids so we never make a big deal of them."

"I gotta get him something."

"No you don't."

"But I will!"

"I know. Thank you!"

Tim took a shower and then started the Subaru, knowing he

should go to the school and start getting his classroom ready for the first day, but instead he drove to the hardware store in nearby Filmore, Wyoming.

It had been the first hardware store he had ever gone to in Wyoming and he'd been surprised to see, next to the hammers and power saws, a collection of guns for sale, too. He saw it as a testament that small-town folks still saw guns as "tools." He knew that buying a strange teenage boy a gun might not be the brightest thing to do, but figured it was something the kid might actually want. The gun range where David had had the scare was not the only place they could go shooting in a county full of open spaces.

Tim debated for a moment as he stared at the display rack. They had a cheap Mossberg Plinkster, next to it a stainless steel Ruger 10/22 with a walnut stock glinted at him from the wall.

A balding clerk approached Tim. "I saw your picture in the paper."

"What?"   –

The clerk turned and picked up a newspaper next to the cash register. He handed it to Tim. A picture of David and Tim staring at the memorial in the cabin rested underneath the headline, "I recognize his voice!"

"You looking for something to hunt this guy down with?" the clerk said, smiling at his own joke.

Tim shook his head without looking up from the article. "I was curious about that Ruger 10/22, when you have a sec." Tim frowned at the page in his hands as he read about David Jenkins having a "psychic ability" that allowed him "to see and hear past events."

Jackson Emmons thinks David's M. Night Shyamalan…

Dread wafted over Tim at the thought of the first day of school, knowing that everyone in town read the stupid paper.

Even kids who made the paper doing conventional things, like sports or speeches, sometimes were teased out of jealousy. He just wished he had thought of that before he'd let Emmons disclose David's name as part of his story.

At least he'll have some fun before the storm hits.

Tim texted Abbey about buying her brother the .22. Then he picked up the rifle from the display counter where the clerk had left it and held the gun to his shoulder, peering through its sights. Abbey's return text buzzed into his cell phone. "Yes, if you teach him how 2 b safe and keep it locked up at your house until he's 18."

Tim slapped his driver's license onto the counter for a background check, along with his credit card and the clerk phoned in the background check.

Driving home, Tim felt the temptation to veer from his course and pop off a couple hundred rounds himself with the walnut beauty. However, it seemed wrong to shoot someone else's gun before they had a chance, like touching their girlfriend or something.

He went home and rested the boxed rifle next to his own on the closet shelf before going to school, where he started unstacking chairs and unpacking some of the books he had ordered over the summer with his own money. They were books he thought the kids might actually like to read, as opposed to the ones that were assigned. He thought it was funny that kids in Wyoming didn't go for Louis L'Amour or Cormac McCarthy or any of the other writers who seemed to fit the bleak landscape. They liked Harry Potter, or Tolkien, and some still liked Encyclopedia Brown instead. He knew some parent might eventually start a fight about the language or other content of some of the books, but if it encouraged the kids to read he'd be willing to argue the case with them. He also made sure to never mark the books with his name and room number as he did the textbooks, so he could always say he had no idea where a kid found that book.

As he razored open his last box of Amazon-supplied novels his phone rang.

"Have you seen David?" Abbey asked.

"Not since our run. Why?"

"He was supposed to meet for lunch at twelve-thirty," she told him.

Tim looked at the clock on the wall. Twelve fifty-six. "He told me he was looking forward to it."

"His phone goes straight to voicemail."

"Maybe his paper route held him up? Do you have a number for Jim or Merv?" Tim asked. "He talked about going over there."

"Merv said that Jim is with him and they haven't seen him."

Tim frowned. "I'm going to go by your house. Maybe he got embarrassed by the article in the paper about him. Will you call me if you see him at Chuck's?"

Tim found the house vacant and jetted over to the burger place, hoping to see David there.

Abbey came out into the parking lot, looking amazing even with a face full of worry. She carried a box wrapped in the funnies from an old newspaper.

"No luck?"

She shook her head.

"Who else does he know?" Tim asked.

"I think Jim and Merv are about it. I even called Merv again, but no one is answering now. I tried his work and they said he picked up his papers this morning."

"Why don't you wait at the house. I'll go see if he's just out delivering."

"Still?"

Tim shrugged. "Maybe he just got held up. Or people stopped to talk to him about being in the paper."

Tim gave her a long hug, then kissed her and smiled, doing his best to reassure her, even though unease was worming through both of them.

Driving towards the newer subdivision south of town where David's paper route was, Tim sweated in the midday heat. The neighborhood was a warren of split-level homes where toys and bicycles splayed over front lawns, abandoned by their owners who now sought shelter from the sun in basement rec rooms. Tim peered through the waves of heat coming up off the asphalt into the distance, hoping the boy would materialize from a mirage and he could call and make Abbey's world right again.

It was easier to focus on that than the creeping sense of fear.

On Tim's right stood an ugly pink house he knew had to be Merv's because people teased him about living in a Pepto-Bismol bottle. Tim parked on the flawless concrete of the driveway and knocked on the door, hoping that he'd find David engrossed in a video game with his friends or playing Dungeons and Dragons or whatever it was kids like them did. Merv answered the door.

"Hey, is David here?"

Merv frowned and shook his head. "We still haven't seen him, Mr. Ross."

"It's cool," Tim said, as he watched Jim bring a spoonful of Jiffy Peanut Butter up from the jar to his mouth on the couch in the living room. "Gimme a call if you see him, okay?" Tim pulled an old receipt out of his wallet and wrote his cell number on the back before handing it to the boy. "Cross-country practice starts Monday at eight-thirty a.m. by the track. I know yer not playing football, so be there!" Tim said over his shoulder as he headed back to his car.

Tim pulled away from the curb and resumed scanning the sidewalks and bramble-filled ditches. After a few minutes of fruitless searching, he called Abbey.

"You find him?" she asked, her voice charged with hope.

"Sorry, but he'll turn up. Why don't you try the school?"

"Okay."

Tim could hear her worry, despite her trying to cover it up.

"What if I call Farner?" he said, pulling over to fish for the business card he had carried in his wallet for days now. "Maybe he went with him."

"If he did, Farner owes me an apology, because David wasn't supposed to go without you!"

"I'll tell him."

A skinny kid rode past Tim on a bicycle and his heart leapt until he realized it was someone else.

"Abbey?"

"Yeah?"

"I love you."

She laughed. "I love you, too, Tim."

"We're going to find him."

"Thanks," she said and hung up.

Part of Tim didn't want to call Farner as he dialed the number off the card. He hoped the cop would simply say, "Oh yeah, he's with me—we're out investigating," and, annoying as that might be, at least they would know the boy was safe. But what he was more afraid of, more certain of even, was that the cop would have no idea where David could possibly be and Tim's best hope would be shattered.

"Hello?"

"This is Tim Ross. You seen David?"

"Not since yesterday."

Tim felt his hopes being crushed somewhere inside him. "Are you cruising around?" he asked.

"Yes, I'm patrolling."

"If you see him will you tell him to call me?"

"Sure," the cop said. "Is everything good?"

"I think so," Tim lied. "It's his birthday and he was supposed to meet up with his sister at noon and people like him aren't usually late. We still haven't seen him."

"Okay," Farner responded, "I'll put a radio call out telling everybody if they see the boy from the paper to contact me immediately, all right?"

"Thank you," Tim said, surprised about the lack of procedure or hoops to jump through.

"We'll look out for him. You can't go far in this town. When he turns up I want you to call me. If he doesn't turn up in an hour or so I'd like you to check in, okay?" Farner said.

"I will. Thank you."

Tim wasn't sure if he felt relieved or more worried now that he had involved the police, just like people do when something really *was* wrong. He called Abbey again to tell her about the police and then began to comb every area where the boy might be in the little town. He scanned the parks, the high school and the playing fields in case Abbey hadn't already. He also drove to the library and looked around, asking the librarians if they had seen him, pointing to David's picture in the newspaper sitting on the checkout counter. He wrote his cell number below the headline, instructing anyone who saw David to call him.

"If he's psychic, can he really be lost, though?" the librarian asked in her old smoker's voice. She began to laugh at her own joke but it only turned into a coughing fit.

Tim left. He called Abbey once more and discovered they

had covered a lot of the same ground.

"We'll find him," Tim said. "Farner may have already located him."

"I'm going to check the bowling alley and recheck the park," Abbey said. "My friend is coming over to wait at the house."

"We'll be laughing about this over Chinese food tonight," Tim said, hearing the lie in his own voice.

"I'd love that," she said before hanging up.

His one day when things should go right—and this is happening!

Street after street, lot after lot turned up empty. The sun had dipped lower in the sky. Every corner Tim turned he hoped to see the kid appear, running with that long champion's gait that hid how awkward he looked the rest of the time. He'd stride up to Tim and tell him he just lost track of time and they'd laugh it off.

Tim would have even settled on seeing David's white running shoes poking through the weeds of a running trail, downed by a sprained ankle or other minor injury that Tim could deal with for him.

I'll fix this! Tim thought, instantly aware that the last time he'd said those words had been back in Iraq, long before he had surrendered to numb fatalism.

***

By 7:00 p.m. another APB had been put out on the boy, referencing his photo in the paper. Tim's search had gone from quietly cruising around to yelling David's name out the open window into the cottonwoods and cattails beside the road that led out into the county as his search widened and grew less targeted.

Tim had also called Mr. Carson, who had agreed to mobilize his VFW buddies to help look.

"Can I tell them you are a Vet?" Carson had asked.

"You can tell them I have two congressional medals of honor if it will help."

"You do?"

"No, but please just say whatever it takes, Mr. Carson!"

Tim's voice had grown raw from yelling for David. Clips and phrases from lurid news stories and made-for-television movies swirled through Tim's brain and threatened to spill over into reality. He had even picked up Grover and let her out of the car along the running path, hoping she would pick up a scent, though she had never been trained to track anything but leftover burgers from Chucks. Grover had simply laid down on the trail and tried to take a nap.

As the sun set Tim stopped by Abbey's house, which had turned into a command post filled with VFWs and police. Erin, Abbey's boss and friend, sat with her, urging her to eat some carry-out pizza.

"They're worried someone might have read the news article and went after David," Abbey said after Tim sat on the couch next to her and wrapped his arms around her.

"Who?"

"Whoever hurt those girls. They might have felt threatened by what they read and gone after him." Her voice started to crack and she swallowed. "I never should have let him go with the police!"

Tim shook his head, hoping to reassure her, but realized he was just trying to ward off his own sense of guilt.

"Maybe he got embarrassed by the news story and is just hiding out for a while," Erin chimed in.

Tim nodded, hoping to comfort Abbey, but he had already

come to similar conclusions to Abbey's. Abbey had just put into words the growing fear he hadn't wanted to consider as he yelled out the window for the boy.

"They're trying to tell me I shouldn't go look for David alone now," Abbey said.

"I'll take you, sweetie," Erin said. "Anything's better than sitting here."

"Thanks, Erin," Tim said. "I'm going to check where David and I go on our runs and see if I can find him out there. I'm going to leave Grover with you. She's too tired to keep up," he added, looking skeptically at the dog resting by the couch as he made for the door. He paused to look Abbey in the eyes. "We'll find him."

Abbey curled the corners of her mouth up for an instant in an attempt at a smile, but it returned to a thin straight line by the time Tim reached the door.

CHAPTER 20

Tim took a flashlight from his car parked in Abbey's driveway and jogged through the trees towards the running path, calling David's name into the dark voids between the tree trunks and tall grass.

He felt a growing sickness at the thought of the boy being taken by whoever had strangled those girls. It didn't matter if David could really see those things or not—if the killer believed he could, or at least believed he might generate interest in what happened, it could be enough for him to hurt David. Tim's anxiety mixed with a sense of shame at letting the boy participate in the investigation in the first place.

As he ran through the darkness, Tim shone his light left and right along the trail. He didn't want to admit it, but he kept pointing it at the ground, looking for the fallen body and gangly limbs of the boy.

Just a sprained ankle.

He didn't want to think about where the boy's phone might be or why it would be turned off. He neared where David probably would have veered from the running path to go to Merv and Jim's neighborhood and stopped to search the ditches, then took off again after finding them empty.

An image had lodged in Tim's head of David lying hurt somewhere. It brought back memories of one of the last times that they had been pulled up to raid a house in Iraq. It had been a place of ornate tiles and clean bedspreads, with a giant flat screen, but after a diligent search they had found a room hidden behind a giant Cherrywood armoire. Lengths of extension cords used as ties trailed like snakes through sticky pools of blood and urine. On a table in the corner, a pair of pliers rested amid broken pieces of dislodged bicuspids and deracinated canines, some with the silver glint of old fillings. It was one of many times Tim had puked in that country.

Following the country road that led out of town, Tim promised himself that if David was not okay he would find whoever hurt him and make them suffer just like the people in that house had.

Still shining his light into the shadows and calling the boy's name, Tim broke free of the aspens and cottonwoods and followed the road onto the wide-open alkali flats where nothing but sagebrush grew.

Up ahead the rounded hills of the gun range glowed a surreal white in the moonlight. Tim hadn't thought to look for the boy there, but now it seemed like as good as any, despite how scared the kid had been of the place.

Tim surged forward a quarter of a mile and then jumped over the cattle guard at the range, taking it like a hurdler. He checked the shooting hut for signs of life then looked out at the warren of canyons and ravines, which were only half visible in the moonlight.

"David!" he called.

Nothing.

He took a deep breath and ran headlong down the dark canyon where he and the kid had played army in what seemed like ages ago.

Why here? Why this place?

Rounding the near hairpin curve to the sound of clay crushing beneath his shoes, he saw the cave. Still there. Silent as a tomb. A mirror image of everything in his nightmare. The light from the moon had pierced into the cavern just deep enough to expose a figure huddled in its depths. Tim came to an abrupt halt.

It's a rock, it's just a–

The rock moved.

"David?" he called, hearing the fear in his own voice.

The figure stood up and Tim saw the outline of a robe spread around its ankles.

"David?"

"Who is that?" a female voice called back.

Tim cursed, thinking of the woman in his nightmares. He started back-pedaling, then stumbled over something and fell. The shards of shattered beer bottles and bullet casings gouged at him through his t-shirt as he rolled onto his side. The figure in the cave descended and moved towards him.

Tim sprang to his feet and sprinted back the way he had come. Then the hum of an engine rattled through the canyon and headlights flared from around the curve ahead. Dodging into one of the crags in the canyon wall at his left so he wouldn't be run down, he saw a jeep zip past him. Its lights fell not on a burqa-clad figure, but on a teenaged girl with long hair and a black dress that went down to her ankles.

The girl waved at the approaching vehicle and jumped down to meet it, smiling. The light from the jeep pierced deep inside the abyss of the cave and caught the reflectors on the girl's bicycle, parked in the shadows of the little cavern. Tim saw nothing else in there and felt himself go slack with relief.

The driver of the jeep got out and the long-haired girl jumped into his arms, wrapping her legs around him in a full-bodied hug. The driver groped the girl's butt and she bit his neck.

If Tim never did find David would the rest of the world continue not to care? Would teenagers still have late-night rendezvous in remote corners like this one? Would everything just keep on going?

As Tim ran his hand over his back to feel for blood, he watched the couple neck in the glow of the headlights. Tim grimaced at the idea of asking them if they had seen David. He didn't expect much of a response. The girl seemed vaguely familiar—he recalled seeing her in the hallways of the school. Tim didn't recognize the giant groping her with his back turned to him, but he wished it could be David, transformed into a Jeep-driving Casanova.

The mesh of arms and legs pivoted as the boyfriend pushed the girl against the Jeep's grille. Suddenly his face became visible in the headlights. It was Al Buoncuore, the guy Tim had kung fu gripped the other day. A guy well into his fifties, yet here he was touching and kissing a girl almost young enough to be his granddaughter.

Tim swore under his breath as he watched the man open his mouth and mash it against the girl's.

"Hey, Buoncuore!" Tim shouted as he stepped away from his spot in the canyon wall. "Whatcha doing?"

Buoncuore jumped with surprise and let the girl go. "Who's that?"

"It's yer pal Tim Ross," Tim said as he advanced on the couple. "What are you doing with a little girl like her?"

"What are *you* doing here?" Buoncuore yelled.

"I'm eighteen!" the girl protested.

"I doubt it!" Tim said, not really caring as he walked toward the Jeep.

"Tim," the big man said slowly, moving toward the sound of Tim's voice in the dark, "this isn't what you think..."

"Never heard that before. Maybe you should keep your tongue in your own mouth and take her home to her grandpa. He'd be about your age!"

"I'm warning you—you need to leave!"

"What are you going to do?" Tim taunted, not in any mood to be threatened.

"Jake, let's just go!" the girl said.

"What did you call him?" Tim asked, startled.

"Ross, if you want to keep your job you're going to turn around and go!"

"You're Jake?" Tim said in shock, half to himself. "Heather Brady's Jake?"

Buoncuore's face went slack in the headlights.

Tim frowned at the man's blank eyes that went as expressionless as a python's just before Buoncuore came at him like a freight train, all two hundred pounds of him. Tim fought the urge to run. The big man closed the last few feet and Tim shot out both hands, gripping the man's polo shirt and putting his own foot against Buoncuore's lower abdomen. At the same time, he rocked back and flexed his hamstring into a bicycle kick that threw the heavy man over himself as he rolled onto his back. Buoncuore splatted into the baked clay of the range.

Before the big man could recover, Tim flipped onto Buoncuore's torso, straddling him, and drove a right hook into the man's jaw. Then he slammed his left fist into Buoncuore's temple and seized the collar of his shirt, twisting it tight over his Adam's apple in an attempt to choke him. Buoncuore's hands shot up, but Tim rammed the butt of his palm across Buoncuore's nose, making a bone-snapping sound. Buoncuore tried to protect his face with his hands as Tim rained more blows on his cheeks and head. He felt his knuckles cut open on something sharp, maybe teeth or the broken bones of Buoncuore's nose, but the pain drowned in the rage coursing through him. Finally he became aware of the coppery smell of blood and of the girl screaming.

"Stop!"

Buoncuore's arms wrapped around his head and he no longer fought back.

"Please!" Her tear stained eyes were wide in the headlights. "He's a good person!"

"Why did you call him Jake?"

"Because he tells me to," she said, sobbing.

"Did you do this with Cassidy Heintz, too?" Tim yelled at the man underneath him.

"Never heard of her," Buoncuore rasped behind his arms.

"She was on the volleyball team, the swimming team and the track team—and you're telling me one of the two athletics directors in such a tiny school district hasn't heard of her?" Tim spat. "The whole town has been looking for her and you've never heard of her?"

"I didn't *know* her... I mean," he gasped.

"Who bought you those clothes?" Tim yelled at the girl.

"He did," the girl said, perhaps thinking that would be in Buoncuore's favor.

"Shut up!" Buoncuore bellowed.

The girl winced.

"Did you ever buy Cassidy Heintz anything? What about Heather Brady? Black and skimpy?" Tim demanded.

"What's he talking about, Jake?" the girl asked tearfully.

"Shut up!" Buoncuore shouted.

"What's your name?" Tim asked the girl.

"Trish."

"Trish, get on your bicycle and go home!"

"What are you going to do to him?"

"I'm going to help him into his Jeep and take him home and get some ice on him."

"He's really not a bad guy," Trish insisted.

"No, of course not," Tim lied, just wanting to get the girl to go and feeling sick at the thought of what the man below him had done. "So please get out of here and somewhere safe and he'll see you after he's healed up. No one has to know."

The crying girl nodded and ran down the beam of the headlights towards her bicycle.

"Get up!" Tim growled, pulling Buoncuore up as he rose off him.

Buoncuore sat up and wobbled like a sideswiped bowling pin. His chest heaved for air.

"Get up!" Tim repeated as Trish mounted her bicycle and swept past them, ashen-faced.

Buoncuore cursed as he gingerly felt his injured face.

"Get up!"

Buoncuore threw back an arm and slowly pushed himself to his feet, looking suddenly much older and heavier.

He glowered at Tim wanting nothing more than to kill this man who had got in the way of what he'd wanted that night. He cocked an arm back with all the speed and grace of a drunk, but before he could drive the fist home, Tim had moved out of sight. He felt the teacher's arm wrapping around his throat from behind and his head being forced down into the crook of Tim's elbow.

"It's a lot easier to choke someone when they're on their feet," Tim whispered coldly.

Buoncuore tried to skitter backward and crush the smaller man against the canyon wall, but Tim's grip only tightened and the big man's panic grew as he struggled to breathe. He flopped and jerked and tried to throw himself to the ground, but that only made it even harder to breathe as the hold grew tighter. The periphery of his vision went dark and shrunk to pinpricks of starlight—and then there was nothing.

CHAPTER 21

Buoncuore's nose throbbed in time to his pulse. It had swollen so much that the bottom half of his vision was cut off. From somewhere far away he could hear the sound of a whistle, like a train or a referee. An orb glowed yellow above his head and he blinked until his eyes focused on the glass of a cheap light covering. He could see two big grey lumps inside it—dead moths that hadn't been cleaned out.

He moved his head forward and felt it explode into sparks and falling stars of pain. Snapping his eyes shut against the hurt, he shifted his gaze from the ceiling to the wall, trying not to move his head. He opened his eyes again and saw tan wallpaper covered with ears of corn and farm plows floating in space.

The whistling sound continued and he recognized it as a tea kettle, its whine loud enough to drill right through his throbbing skull.

Something had been wrapped around his mouth, something painfully tight. He wanted to touch his face, but grew vaguely aware he couldn't move his arms. Was he paralyzed? He slumped his head to the left, risking more pain, and peered down at his torso. He was wrapped in duct tape around what felt like a computer chair.

Buoncuore flinched as he heard footsteps behind him on what sounded like kitchen linoleum. He felt someone's eyes burrowing into the back of his neck as he held perfectly still, as if by not moving he could somehow blend in with his surroundings.

The person behind him snorted. Then he heard the kettle

being taken off the burner. Another metallic rattle he didn't recognize sounded and then a tinging noise came as if something was being placed on a spoon rest.

Buoncuore tried to work out what was going on. He was injured and someone was nursing him with tea?

He detected the slight noise of a mug being removed from a cupboard and then he heard it being filled with liquid. Then Tim Ross appeared in front of him, holding a mug in his right hand. He sat down in a kitchen chair facing him.

"You drink tea?" Tim asked, lifting the cup towards his captive as if it were the most natural thing in the world to offer tea to someone you had beaten up and tied to a chair in your kitchen.

Buoncuore shook his head then felt the pain again.

"You know I don't either," Tim said, shaking his head sorrowfully. "Guess you're more of a coffee guy. Were you drinking coffee when you read this morning's paper?" Tim asked leaning in slightly.

Buoncuore stared but didn't say anything.

"Did you read the headline about a skinny teenaged kid finally shedding some light on who's been making all these girls disappear over the years?"

Tim studied the man's eyes. He saw no response in them, which in fact said a lot. He shook his head and set his cup on the kitchen table untouched, then stood up to walk behind Buoncuore.

"I thought I had some of those hot cocoa packets around here somewhere. I stole them from the hotel during the last teachers' conference up in Jackson, but..."

The captive heard the sound of the tea kettle being lifted and then felt something warm next to his right cheek. Buoncuore's eyes widened in horror as he saw the steaming bright-red pot less than half an inch from his face.

"How many quarts do you think this holds?" Tim asked as he slowly moved it back and forth in front of Buoncuore's battered face. "You wanna take a guess?" Tim passed it casually from one hand to the other less than an inch from Buoncuore's face. The long handle bumped against his broken nose, making the big man whimper in agony.

"I would say… I dunno… how many quarts are there in a gallon?" Tim asked as he strolled behind the man's back with the kettle.

Buoncuore cringed, the image of steaming liquid pouring down his spine seared through his brain.

"One thing's for sure," Tim said, crouching down and putting his face in Buoncuore's, "it sure is hot." He wiggled his fingers in the rising steam and withdrew them quickly.

Without warning, Tim slammed his forehead right against Buoncuore's and thrust the open pot close against his chest.

"How many of these pots am I going to have to pour on your balls before you tell me where David Jenkins is?" he hissed.

Some of the water in the pot spilled out and rolled down Buoncuore's chest and belly. Buoncuore jerked and made a noise like a wolf howling at the moon, muffled by his gag.

"You gonna tell me?" Tim shouted, holding the open pot over the man's face poised to pour it on him.

Buoncuore nodded frantically through his tears.

Tim lowered the pot and set it on the stove. Then he produced a paring knife from the kitchen rack and cut the tape from Buoncuore's mouth, taking little care not to nick him in the process.

Buoncuore gasped and heaved for breath. Then he licked his lips, moistening them with a disgusting slathering sound.

"Where is he?" Tim demanded.

Buoncuore shook his head. "I dunno," he said in a hoarse and ragged tone.

"You don't know!" Tim said, thrusting his own nose against Buoncuore's broken one, eyes ablaze like a methed-up drill sergeant. "You don't know?"

Buoncuore shook his head.

"Your Jeep is full of duct tape and zip ties and two pairs of handcuffs and you don't know?"

Buoncuore shook his head again and Tim felt a rage like he had never felt before, not even in Iraq. He rocketed a clenched fist across the side of Buoncuore's face and moved like a serpent to the stove.

Buoncuore screamed as his sinuses filled with blood. He tried to turn in his chair to see Tim. A moment later he recoiled as the pointed end of a twisted wire coat hanger glowed crimson an inch from his eye.

"I'm going to shove this right into your eye until your brain comes out as steam," Tim growled holding the coat hanger with a blue-and-white checked pot holder. "So you better tell me where that kid is!"

Buoncuore felt the heat from the hanger radiate onto his eyelid, and he could almost feel it singe his eyelash.

"Tim!" Buoncuore stammered trying to inch away from the glowing prong. "Tim, I don't know where he is, but he's dead!"

Buoncuore felt the white-hot metal bite into the flesh of his eyebrow and he screamed, lurching backward as the chair tipped over onto the floor of the kitchen.

The shock of what Buoncuore had said roared through every cell in Tim's body. He kicked the fallen man in the stomach and loomed menacingly over him.

"How do you know he's dead, but don't know where he is?" he shouted, throwing the hot metal hanger at Buoncuore, only for it to bounce off him.

"What difference does it make where he is, Ross?" Buoncuore yelled. "He's dead!"

Tim kicked Buoncuore again, this time in the ribs. The big man let out a shriek. Tim stepped over his victim and left the room.

Buoncuore waited on the cold floor, thankful that his assailant had left, but his bladder nearly voided when Tim stepped back into the room carrying a gleaming revolver.

"If you don't tell me where he is, then you are no good to me!" Tim said coldly, standing over his victim.

He pointed the fat .357 at Buoncuore. The terrified captive became faintly aware of the creeping wetness of urine between his thighs.

Tim cocked the hammer.

"Wait!" Buoncuore screamed.

Tim fired.

A mind-numbing bang, as deafening as artillery in the confined space of the kitchen erupted as the bullet spiraled out of the short-barreled pistol at the speed of sound.

Buoncuore slowly opened his eyes. Tim reached down and jerked him, still tied to the chair, onto his side so he could see the hole the slug had torn in the floor a couple of feet away from his head.

"That's going to be you if you don't tell me where David Jenkins is."

"You kill me and you'll never know."

Tim shrugged. "I kill you and we're all better off."

Tim opened the revolver and shook out the bullets. The spent shell casing landed on the floor by the hole, which emitted a single white ribbon of smoke. He picked a single live round up. Holding it between thumb and forefinger, he tapped it on Buoncuore's forehead.

"Look at me!" Tim hissed through the buzzing in their ears from the gunshot.

Buoncuore refused.

Tim tapped the bridge of Buoncuore's nose with the heavy revolver and the man's eyelids flickered with pain. Tim rolled him onto his back.

"You see this?" he challenged, holding up the big bullet he had plucked from the floor. "It's a .357 Magnum. Same caliber, same kind as before. Primer on the butt, jacketed hollow point on the tip," he said, showing both ends of the bullet to the terrified man.

"This is *not* a blank!" he informed his captive, slamming it into the revolver's cylinder and clacking it shut. Then he pushed the snub-nosed barrel right between Buoncuore's eyebrows where he could feel the heat from the last firing against his skin. "And this time I won't have room to miss."

He spun the revolver's chambers with the gun still pointed at the bound man. "One bullet, six chambers. You want to tell me where David is? It all stops and I leave you alone. You don't and one in six becomes one in five, one in four… the odds just get worse if it doesn't kill you on the first shot. You ready?" Tim gave him a nasty smile.

Buoncuore shook his head.

"Then tell me where he is! You're getting better odds than you ever gave any of those little girls," Tim added coldly. "Firing on three."

The big man gave no sign of regret or remorse, none of the signs of contrition Tim would have paid good money to see.

"One." Tim didn't want to kill again, but the thought of Buoncuore murdering one of the few people he had felt close to in years made him tighten his grip on the pistol.

"Two!" Tim yelled. He knew he had backed himself into a corner, that the first shot could vaporize any chance of ever finding David's remains. But if Buoncuore wasn't going to tell, even after being beaten and burned, at least it would stop the murders and David would be avenged.

"Three!" Tim spat. He flexed his grip ready for the recoil and tensed his trigger finger to send the piece of human garbage below him to whatever waited for him on the other side they both hoped didn't exist.

A cold hand, as frosty as an ice block and as soft as satin, landed on Tim's shoulder. It radiated a blood-freezing chill through Tim's sweat-soaked t-shirt, through his skin, through his muscles and all the way down to the marrow of his bones. The touch of death.

Tim's buddies had sometimes sworn they had seen the scythe-swinging predator of the battlefield when they had been up on watch for too many nights. He looked to his right, certain that he would finally see the worst thing even someone with his experiences could see. He expected to be confronted by a void inside the hood of the black cloak where a face would be, bone-white hands pushing him aside to reap the soul he'd been sent for, but instead he saw... her.

Aunt Jenny.

Her hand on his shoulder felt reassuring as his mother's, despite its chill. The desperate look he had seen in her eye when she had appeared to him, the crazy look he had detected in the photos of her, were now replaced by a resigned peace. As if the odd expressions she had worn were now smoothed over.

She looked down at the gun in his right hand. She pursed her lips and shook her head as if warning a child about something.

Tim moved the pistol and then he followed the woman's eyes down to Buoncuore. The big man's mouth spread agape, his eyes wide. He could clearly see her as well. Jenny frowned at him, not in hatred or vengeance, but in pity. She took a knee next to the bound man and reached for his face.

"Don't touch me!" Buoncuore screamed.

The man's eyes widened as he felt the freezing hand on his cheek and saw the woman's expression become angry. She lowered her face to his, teeth bared in rage. She stuck out two fingers bearing long cracked fingernails with chipped pink polish before she began pushing them into Buoncuore's eye sockets.

"He's in my basement!" Buoncuore shrieked through closed eyes as the nails gouged into his eyelids. The rictus-mouthed victim of his crimes withdrew her nails and looked up at Tim. Her grimace softened as she stepped back and frowned at Tim before sighing and fading into nothing.

CHAPTER 22

Tim shot out of his door with the gun still in his hand, hoping that Aunt Jenny would come back and do her worst to the man duct-taped to the chair in his kitchen.

He jumped into the Subaru, tossing the gun onto the passenger seat, and slammed it into reverse. Just then Officer Farner's patrol car pulled up in front of him and blocked the drive. Tim burst out of the car and ran to the cop, hurriedly exiting his own car.

"You okay?" the policeman asked. "Someone called saying they heard a shot and screaming."

"I know where David is!" Tim shouted.

Deputy Farner's face lit up.

"My back door is unlocked. Al Buoncuore's in there—he's your guy!"

A startled Farner grabbed the microphone from his shoulder and started speaking rapidly into it. Tim ran back to the Subaru and drove onto the lawn and over the sidewalk to jet past the cop's car.

Tim had been to Buoncuore's just once, for a New Year's party he threw for the teachers, a nice place in the town's newest subdivision. Tim hurtled at top speed through residential streets.

It made no difference that the boy had probably been broken, bloodied and killed—Tim would hold the remains of the last real friend he had made in the world before the punishment for what he had done to that perverted slob in his kitchen came down on him.

He threw the door of the car open and ran to the front door

of the split level.

Locked!

It was quite possibly the only door in all of Uinta County that was bolted.

That should be proof enough.

Tim braced himself and drove his foot hard against the middle of the door. It gave, but not all the way. He cursed and kept kicking until the door jamb itself splintered and gave way for him to rush inside.

A warm and distant wave of remembrance washed over him as he entered the split-level. He half expected to find himself back in the terracotta of those Iraqi houses, to feel the odd stony coolness they provided in spite of the heat, to hear the rapid chatter of Arabic as peoples' homes were raided. Instead, Tim saw only the modern, hyper-clean home of Albert Buoncuore when he flicked on the lights. The walls and furnishings radiated an untainted, antiseptic quality that hit you with the odor of a hundred little rearview mirror pine trees. It felt to Tim that if he went through every thread of the bushy new carpet he would find no dirt, no hair, not a trace of life. Not a scrap of DNA.

"David!" Tim shouted, his voice sounding like a burned-out bullhorn by now. "David!"

No response.

Tim moved left after sweeping to his right with the pistol for the slightest sign of movement of any potential accomplice Buoncuore might have. Then he descended the steps leading to the partial basement on his left. No one was with him to watch his back or help him return fire. He burst into the long hallway and swatted the light switch at the bottom of the stairs, ready for action. No one was there.

"David!" Tim yelled again. His heart sank when there was

no reply.

He ran down the hall and shouldered through the half-open door of the first room, sweeping his weapon from left to right. No one. Just a pool table, an old big-screen TV, and a few couches. He whirled around and charged the door opposite the rec room. It flung open before him where he found a blue-themed guest bedroom. The bed had been neatly made and was void of David or anyone else. He searched the empty closet and his heart began to sink.

At the end of the hall, he could see a bathroom sink behind the door. He charged in, calling David's name. Nothing. He whirled around and pushed open the last door in the basement, hammering the light switch. A single bulb flickered in a dimly lit workroom. Screwdrivers and hammers hung from the walls and saws lined the workbenches in perfect order. There wasn't so much as a grain of sawdust out of place.

"David!" Tim yelled at the top of his lungs. His voice cracked with desperation and he felt his heart breaking. He had gone this long, made it this far, from Iraq to Phoenix and through the desperate hot days of this last terrible summer, keeping his guard up, ever ready... and now he felt the whole world starting to collapse on him.

Buoncuore had lied.

"David!" he yelled once more, though he knew that the boy would never hear his name being called.

Tim imagined the Iraqi woman whom he had shot laughing at him, pointing at him with her left hand and tossing her head back, not in screaming agony, or terror, but in deep-bellied reverberating laughs that showed all her missing teeth. The bullet hole in her head oozing and dripping something thick and red between her mocking eyes.

This was what happened to people like Tim—people who

did their best, but ended up doing something so horrible that no matter what it would always catch up with them. Because of their past and their misdeeds, the horror would come upon all those they loved and had dared to get close to.

Tim's chest heaved and he sobbed. He wanted to call Abbey, but he didn't want to tell her that he had failed.

The police would have found Al by now. Even though Buoncuore had deserved what Tim did to him, he would probably have to go to jail. He stared at the pistol and felt the world move heavy and slow beneath him.

It's over.

The dying thought he always imagined soldiers had when a blast or a bright white flash of shrapnel said that it was done.

The cops would be here any minute.

Tim opened the cylinder on the gun. The lone bullet he'd loaded into the .357 rested in position to be struck by the hammer. Buoncuore would not have survived even one round of Russian roulette had Aunt Jenny not come. He clacked the gun shut before cocking the hammer.

He took a breath and slowly raised the gun to his temple. He'd never pointed a gun at himself before. It made him feel sick and dizzy. He imagined that day in the pool when he had thought of just sinking to the bottom of its twelve feet.

Just go limp. Sink down and let your finger curl around the trigger as you fall.

His finger shook inside the trigger guard. Just six pounds of pressure and it would all be over, no consequence for what he had done to Buoncuore. No more guilt for all the people he had failed. No more visits from that Iraqi woman who ripped through his nightmares and made him want to die when he woke.

He closed his eyes and inhaled.

One last breath.

He opened his eyes.

One last look.

The street light burning outside the basement window gave the metal of the tools along the wall a blue glow. That was when he noticed the brand-new padlock on the hasp of a small corner closet.

He thought again of how he just wanted it all to be over, but in spirit of crossing all the "t's" and leaving no stone unturned before he ended it, he laid the cocked gun on the workbench and grabbed a crowbar from Buoncuore's tools, shoved it underneath the hasp and slid a block of wood under the bar for leverage.

"David!" he shouted, working on the bar as the wood popped and splintered and the hasp's screws tore from the frame. Tim wrenched open the closet door. David's gangly frame, still clad in his running clothes, lay on the floor in the cramped, sweltering space.

CHAPTER 23

The coffin weighed more than Tim thought it would. For someone well acquainted with death, for someone who had lost his best friend to war, it was strange that he hadn't been to a funeral before, let alone be a pallbearer. Out of respect for the dead, Tim had shined, lint-rolled and pressed every square millimeter of his dress uniform. He would start today to make up for the things he had failed so miserably at in his life. Cleaning the buttons on his jacket with a Q-tip he finally realized why Abbey was such a neat freak. When your world is chaos you do the best you can to fix, to remedy, to control and to improve what you can. Maybe he could polish away some of the scars of his messy past.

In a weird way, it must have been the same for Al Buoncuore and his ultra-clean house. He must have felt, on some level, a little weird, "a little off," about what he did, so he had taken to controlling his environment, his domain, his chunk of the world, with Mr. Clean and Scrubbing Bubbles.

On command Tim and the other pallbearers lowered the coffin into the grave. After they were dismissed, he took his seat next to Abbey crying her eyes out. Wrapping his hand around her own, he put his arm around her shoulders. Everyone stared down at the casket before them. Mr. Carson, the eternal teacher and veteran, lay inside wearing a charcoal suit with his hands crossed over his chest. He had been found slumped at the wheel of his ancient truck, dead of a heart attack as he helped search for David.

When Tim discovered David in the filthy, windowless little room in Buoncuore's house, he picked up the limp body reeking of sweat and pee and fear, and screamed David's name into the kid's closed eyes. David was still warm—hot, in fact, and covered with grimy perspiration.

"C'mon, buddy!" Tim urged, reaching for the boy's jugular to check his pulse.

The boy groaned and attempted to open his eyes.

Still breathing. Still beating.

He rushed the boy in his arms upstairs and began to run cold water over his face and head from the spray hose on the kitchen sink. The kid stuck his tongue out to lap at the stream of water going over his face.

After the boy started to drink, Tim laid him on the cool linoleum floor and grabbed a water bottle from the fridge. He carefully let the boy nurse from it, lying on his side, then called 911 and requested an ambulance.

"I thought you were dead!" Tim said to the boy in a trembling voice.

The kid blinked and nodded like a sleepy infant.

"I'm not letting you go. You're going to make it!"

The boy's eyes revolved lazily in their sockets and stared up at Tim. His lips slowly curled into a grin and then he went back to drinking water.

Tim felt relieved when the EMTs arrived. After desperately searching for a vein in the boy's thin, parched arms they managed to start giving him a saline solution.

Tim called Abbey after they started working on the boy. It was the best feeling in his life to tell her he'd found David alive.

Farner caught up with Tim and Abbey at the hospital in Evanston. Tim hoped fervently that they wouldn't take him away from the boy until he could see him rise and walk again. Farner met Tim's defeated gaze at David's bedside, looking all business, as if a pair of handcuffs was only moments away, but after watching him and Abbey for a while the cop took pity on him.

"You aren't going anywhere, are you?" he asked.

Tim shook his head.

They released David from the hospital two days later, tired and muddy-headed, but oddly good-natured about the whole thing. After coming home Tim had made up the couch in his living room like a bed and put the boy in it so he could watch all the movies and play all the video games he wanted. Tim himself now wore his pistol in his waistband, ever ready to confront anyone or anything who might threaten David again.

That first night Tim and Abbey slept on the living room floor within a few feet of the sleeping child. Grover rested by the front door as added security.

The next morning Captain Yates appeared in the doorway of Tim's house. He looked tired and broken.

"Can I have a word with you?" he asked, his eyes tired and sagging like those of a Saint Bernard.

The two men sat somewhat awkwardly on the cheap porch swing that had come with the rental. Tim felt nervous, but assumed that if he was going to be arrested, no cop would want to be so informal as to sit next to him on a swing.

Yates held the wide brim of his hat in his hand and the two stared out at the last summer cottonwood seeds blowing across the asphalt of the street. It made Tim's nose itch.

"Why were you out at the gun range?" the cop asked.

"It was the only place I hadn't looked yet. I retraced the route David likes to run and thought maybe I should look there."

The cop nodded thoughtfully. "We have a videotaped statement made by Patrisha Meadows. Do you know her?"

"The name sounds familiar," Tim said wondering what this was about.

"She's the high school student you caught with Al Buoncuore," Yates explained. "Tim, I think she must be the dumbest kid I've ever met. After we busted Buoncuore, she comes by wanting to see him and then of course we ask her why. Because we knew what Buoncuore had been up to, we quickly got her to spill the beans on what they'd been doing. We got her on tape saying what happened at the range the other night that you caught them. How you tried to intervene and Buoncuore attacked you and you gave him a beating."

Tim nodded. "He was fooling with a teenaged girl. I told him to stop and he charged me like a bull."

The cop nodded. "If anyone asks you, or asks us, how that inbred split his nose open and got all banged up, you'll tell them that's when it happened, right? When you fought?"

"That's right," Tim confirmed. "Mostly."

"No, not mostly. Exactly," Yates said, staring intensely at him. "No matter what you hear, what people say, your contact with Mr. Buoncuore ended after you drove him to the police station after your fight, where we arrested him and he said that David was in his basement because he knew that it was all over."

"Right."

Yates stared out into the vacant street again, his fingers rubbing the fabric of his hat.

"A month or two ago I would have arrested you," he said flatly. "You'd be right across the aisle from where we've got Buoncuore." He licked his lips before continuing. "But that was before someone ripped away one of the most valuable things I've ever come to know and strangled the life out of her. We know what you did in there." Yates cocked his head over his shoulder towards the house. "I don't want to know how you came up with that, if you learned it in Iraq, or just out of necessity…" He looked back now at a lazy cyclone of cotton pods caught in an updraft. "I just worry that I would have done a lot worse now that I know how it feels."

The cop sat for a while longer in silence before he finally strode away from the house towards his cruiser.

"Take care of those people," Yates called back, pointing at the house where Abbey and David were.

"What about Buoncuore?" Tim called back.

"Dead," Yates said stopping and turning to Tim. "Hanged himself in his cell. Kept talking about his eyes and how she was going to come for them. Kept going on and on all night, started screaming that she was back and he didn't want to be alone then we found him soon after." Yates stopped to suck his teeth for a second. "Vince Roy is my cousin on the Yates's side. He's the county coroner." He stared at Tim as if gauging to see if he was catching his drift. "He hasn't been real thorough with a guy who we all know died of asphyxiation from a bed sheet."

"What about Farner?" Tim asked.

"He's blaming himself about what happened to David, releasing his name and everything. He feels so bad he's not going to say anything different to what we've talked about."

Yates got into his cruiser and backed out of the driveway.

CHAPTER 24

The next few days were like Christmas for Tim and the Jenkins. They spent a lot of time in their pajamas, watching movies, playing board and video games, roughhousing with Grover and ordering out for pizza. Tim made amazing breakfasts on which they would graze throughout the day. Everything from waffles, omelets and chorizo to scrambled eggs and French toast. David's appetite slowly returned.

The kid was surprisingly open about what had happened.

"I was doing my paper route when Mr. Buoncuore pulled up next to me in his Jeep and asked if I wanted a ride. I told him I'd rather run, but then he told me to get in for a second 'cause he wanted to talk to me about cross-country. I shouldn't have gotten in," he admitted, embarrassed, as he picked over a small helping of one of Tim's potato and egg skillets.

"David, he abused your trust," Abbey told him. "Some weird person wants you or me to get in their car we'd tell them to get lost, but Buoncuore had an unfair advantage."

They had to repeat this like a mantra to David several more times to stop him from blaming himself for what had happened. After getting in the Jeep Buoncuore had pointed a small .22 pistol at David's belly and drove him to his house, where he forced him through the garage into his basement.

"What did he say to you?" Tim asked.

"Not much. He shouted things at me through the door in that little room. He knew from the paper about me helping the police so he kept messing with me, saying 'where's your ghost now!' Things like that. Then he started to ask me to pick lottery numbers and predict baseball scores. I told him I don't do that kind of thing and he said I had better start. So I picked a few. I don't even really know what a normal baseball score is or what the teams are so he threw a sports page in there with me so I could get an idea."

"He wanted to make you a psychic slave?" Tim asked incredulously.

David shrugged. "I guess he was going to give it a shot anyway."

"Did he hurt you?" Abbey asked, pursing her lips in anger.

"No, not really. He just tried to scare me mostly." David bit his lip thoughtfully. "I think he was going to kill me in the end, though."

The phrase went down like a lead weight at the breakfast table.

"I mean, there's no way I would have kept quiet if he let me go and though he scared me I wouldn't have shut up once I got out of there. I heard him placing bets on the phone with someone and then later on he said that if my numbers came in he'd keep me around. Then he didn't come back."

It sounded just like Buoncuore, Tim thought, to be teasing and jovial, yet needing to be in control, edged with the potential for sadism and violence.

After breakfast Tim called Jackson Emmons and asked him to come over.

The journalist and the little group Tim now thought of as his family sat on the couches staring at each other.

"You know that David could have been killed because of what you wrote, right?" Tim asked.

"You guys gave permission for him to be interviewed," Emmons said quietly. "Everything I wrote was true."

"If you had known this was going to happen to him, would you still have written the article?"

Emmons looked down at Grover resting in the doorway. "No."

Tim nodded approvingly. "You got some good headlines because of David, now can you do him a favor?"

Emmons shrugged.

"Can you write a part two and make sure he comes off as the bravest, toughest fifteen-year-old in Wyoming?"

"What about freedom of the press?" said Emmons, smirking.

"What about it?" Tim smirked back. "No one's holding a gun to your head, but can you at least try?"

***

The headline came out before the first day of school: "Heroic Teen's Ordeal."

"Even I think that's a little over the top," David said as they ate lunch together after their run.

The article was everything Tim wanted. When school started the next day, everyone saw the awkward, gangly boy in a new light. The teasing he now received was fairly good-natured and the one punk who went out of his way to harass David felt the wrath of one of the jocks looking eagerly to redeem their school's reputation. No one argued against the accusations against Buoncuore, but everyone felt shocked and ashamed.

Tim couldn't help but miss the old wrangler-clad veteran he had spent his lunches with in the teachers' lounge. He almost felt guilty about missing him, but he thought petty pains and sadness were what helped people be normal again after something traumatic. In honor of his friend he joined the VFW the second week of school.

The Meadowlark High School's new running team had their first cross-country meet two weeks later, arranged for them by Tim. David's showing was absurd. Tim knew the boy could move, but the kid ran three miles in just over fourteen minutes at six thousand feet above sea level. The gangly nerd of Meadowlark High had found the one thing he proved exceptional at.

"You've been holding out when we run, huh?" Tim asked on the ride home.

The boy didn't respond, but Tim saw him grin lopsidedly from his spot in the passenger seat.

"Were you holding out today?" Tim joked.

"Yeah," the boy said frankly.

That jarred Tim. The fastest he had ever heard of anyone killing off three miles was around twelve and a half minutes.

"It was my first race and I didn't want to get screwed, didn't want to mess up my pacing." He paused to sip from his strawberry shake. "But, yeah, I'll go faster next time."

There was no bravado, no bragging, just fact.

***

David placed first in the varsity race at State in Casper, Wyoming. It was late October by then and thankfully the evil summer had finally dropped dead. Everyone looked forward to the first snowfall of the year in the little mountain town.

David began to repeatedly call a tall thin blonde girl from Kemmerer, Wyoming who he'd met at a cross-country invitational. She had strong cheekbones and a cute smile and, after a lot of teasing from Tim, David had finally said "hi" to her. She took over from there and revealed that she was a quiet but dedicated fan of the now tanned, wiry oddball who had killed the competition and set a new state record. She spent a lot of time in Meadowlark with David, which meant Abbey and Tim now had more time alone together.

After the first snow, Tim finally pulled the Ruger 10/22 from his closet shelf. He called David, who at that moment was frantic to see his girlfriend but was unable to because the roads to and from Kemmerer sixty miles to the north, remained closed due to blowing snow.

"Quit talking to her for an hour or two and come with me," Tim told him. "I have something to give you."

He picked David up and the two went to the gun range which unlike the road to Kemmerer, remained still and windless. Tim presented him with the rifle.

"So this is like a late birthday, timely state champ, early best man present," Tim said.

David took the rifle and stared at it with all the reverence and fascination Tim had hoped for. He gave Tim the smile that always made him so happy, but this time it actually stayed on his face for more than a moment.

"Best man?" David asked.

"Yeah. I want you to be my best man."

"When?"

"December."

David adjusted the sights on the gun, following Tim's instructions, and began consistently pinging the metal target down-range.

"You still want to join the army?" Tim asked.

"Yeah," David said. "I'm already getting calls from different colleges because of the record in Casper, but I'm wondering about West Point."

"They'll want runners, I'm sure," Tim told him.

"Karen said she'd miss me, though."

"I will, too," Tim said, embarrassed by his sudden honesty.

David glanced away from his sights and studied Tim.

Tim cleared his throat uncomfortably. "You should still go, though."

David nodded and looked back down his sights at the target. Then he lowered his gun. His eyes were fixed on something down-range. For the first time in months Tim saw the same old David, the dreamy-eyed, pseudo-psychic David. He followed his gaze.

Walking over the snow, that glowed gold in the setting sun, was Aunt Jenny. She seemed unaware of the two men as she moved quietly over the thick drifts in her Christmas sweater. She walked across their line of fire and towards the side canyon where Tim had fought with Buoncuore.

"You see her?" David asked.

Tim nodded and felt the hair stand up all over his body.

"I've seen her down in that cave beyond the curve in my nightmares," Tim whispered as they continued to watch her. He hesitated as she disappeared into the mouth of the canyon before going on. "When I slept, I used to see a lady I killed in Iraq down there. Then I started seeing Aunt Jenny with a baby."

"She had a baby?" David asked.

Tim nodded, realizing he had just admitted what had happened in Iraq to the boy and that somehow the world continued to move.

"Whose baby do you think it was?" David asked.

***

It made Tim sick when he thought about how close he'd come to killing Buoncuore, not for Buoncuore's sake, but because he'd almost terminated the one link that led him to David in time.

As the days passed, Tim had come to think of Aunt Jenny as their patron saint. She was a phantom that had come back from the dead to protect her kin and scare Buoncuore into telling Tim where her nephew was being held.

After Tim saw her waft over the newly fallen snow of the gun range and glide towards the canyon, it became fairly clear in his mind what had happened to Aunt Jenny.

Tim and David had to drive all the way to the truck stop on the I-80 to find a working payphone from which they called the police department. Tim left an anonymous tip about a murder victim being buried under the ledge that formed the cave in the canyon. Neither Tim nor David wanted any more involvement with the police.

Months after the exhumation of three different female corpses buried in the tiny cave, forensic experts completed reconstructing their faces. However, long before a completely positive ID could be made, the police were highly suspicious that one of the skeletons, found lying in the tatters of a tacky red Christmas sweater, was probably that of Jenny. Her "missing" photo showed her wearing the same sweater found in her grave.

Forensics showed that she was in fact very pregnant when she died.

"Maybe that was why she wore those crazy sweaters. She was trying to hide her baby," Abbey concluded gloomily as they read about it in the paper after the identity had been confirmed through DNA.

CHAPTER 25

One Friday after school, Tim returned to the library and pulled a handful of yearbooks from the shelf. He sat in a corner, thumbing through them. Snow steadily dropped in sheets outside and it felt good to sit in the quiet. After searching around, he found the sophomore and junior pictures of Aunt Jenny. He saw, even in her somewhat addled state, that she made a big deal out of the pictures. She wore a lot of very bright make-up and big dangly earrings. The earrings in the sophomore picture looked like bananas, while in the junior photo they were just simple gold hoops. Her hair was always meticulously feathered.

Looking at all the pictures of the other kids felt slightly creepy, knowing what they might conceal. It was as if their smiles or glares for the yearbook photographer were just facades behind which there might be a spider web of hidden tragedies and scandals.

Tim skimmed forward to Buoncuore's photo. His picture and his name first appeared in the yearbook of Jenny's junior year, which had been when he had returned to the small town and started teaching at Meadowlark High School. Buoncuore had a thick, jutting jaw and sported greasy hair that flowed down over his tweed jacket. He wore a striped button-up shirt with one of those disgusting bolo ties that looked like a boot lace wrapped around a rock. His smile was as wide as a crocodile's but it didn't travel north of his nose. It was the smile you see on the faces of car salesmen or politicians or other people with an agenda.

Jackson Emmons, with whom Tim now exchanged increasingly friendly barbs at the grocery store, VFW Hall and wherever else they happened to meet, busily drafted a book about "The Meadowlark Killer" and had given Tim a copy of the manuscript to fact check.

Emmons posited the idea that Jenny Jenkins might have been Buoncuore's first victim, and even took the license to describe a scene of innocent flirtation between the handsome new teacher and a girl who was too old for her grade. It conjectured that something had started between the two and had then just spiraled out of control.

According to Emmons' articles in *The Meadowlark Call*, two of the three corpses had been identified as different girls suspected of having run away over the decades. The third remained a Jane Doe. She may have been someone Buoncuore had picked up. The mass grave in the cave had grown too full of bodies and he had begun to deposit his victims in old cabins and abandoned houses throughout the county.

Tim and David concurred that the trauma of Aunt Jenny being attacked at the gun range by Mortensen and Brinker had been enough to seal the incident to the spot and allow David to see it, even though she hadn't been killed by them. It was just a coincidence that she was killed only a few hundred yards away not long after.

Further questioning of Trish Meadows, if reliable, proved she had only recently begun her activity with Buoncuore. Perhaps Heintz had been discarded in favor of Trish.

Tim leaned back against the wall of the darkened library and stared up at the ceiling. He wanted to go home, to set the yearbook down and walk away to be with Abbey and David in front of the fire during the storm, but one thought persisted stubbornly in his mind.

He, too, was a killer. He, too, had killed an innocent person.

It might be true that his motivations were different, that war made things different, a fact that he told himself every day. It had been an "understandable accident." However, the awful fact remained that somewhere, in a grave in the dust and sand and sediment, a woman's body moldered because of what he had done. Just like the girls, Buoncuore had lain in the earth. Tim would imagine Al Buoncuore obsessing over what he had done after the first time he had committed murder. He sensed the guilty reality of it looming over him when he ate alone in his house, whispering to him in the dark when he tried to sleep. In that respect, Tim wasn't that different from the murderer.

For weeks after reading Jackson's manuscript, Tim had read avidly about serial killers, studying Anne Rule and Robert Ressler and countless true crime and Wikipedia articles. He tried to establish whether Buoncuore was a natural-born killer. He wasn't a soldier or a Marine trained to kill, but had he been literally born, forged in the womb, to be a psychopath as some research suggested? Tim wanted desperately to believe there could be something that separated him from killers like the man in the yearbook.

He went so far as to pose as a journalist and call old family members of Buoncuore still living in Meadowlark. He phone interviewed classmates and even Buoncuore's boxing coach in Utah. Tim's findings were that something was in fact "sorta screwy" with Buoncuore long before he ever hurt the girls exhumed at the gun range and elsewhere. However, the more Tim learned about the man, the more human Buoncuore became, and that bothered him.

If Tim kept on living with what he had done, if he lived like a normal happy person just as Buoncuore had, did it make him just as bad?

He looked away from the crocodilian grin of Albert Buoncuore's yearbook picture and watched skiffs of snow spin and swirl in the parking lot outside, where the school buses had already picked up. He finally closed the yearbook and resolved never to open it again. Then he walked home through the blowing snow.

***

Tim awoke in the old familiar movie set of his dream. However, this time it wasn't burning hot.

The gun range clay he walked over shone free of shell casings and broken glass. The ground was pristine white, like the sand on a beach in the south Pacific. The clay crushed softly beneath his feet, which were now shod in a pair of sandals.

He knew he was dreaming. He knew it was August again and another record high in Meadowlark, but the heat didn't bother him as badly as it used to.

He walked along the canyon to where the burqa woman sat calmly inside the cave. In spite of the cool, the sun illuminated everything in the box canyon as brightly as a searchlight on a wedding cake. Everything appeared vivid and hyper-real. Even the cave no longer remained darkened and he could see all the way to its back wall.

He approached the burqa woman respectfully, still not able to see her eyes.

"Hello," he said.

She made no response.

"I threw the medal they gave me after what happened into the ocean when we went to Oregon last June." He wasn't sure if that would mean anything to her. "Maybe it'll end up in Iraq again. I dunno, but I don't have it anymore."

Still no response.

"You know that I've put it behind me." He paused, feeling calm in spite of the weight of what he said. "Mostly anyway..." He bit his lips for a moment. "What happened was wrong, but I wouldn't have done it had I known more. I can't bring you back, but I've also learned that I can't fix what happened by ruining what's left."

A soft breeze played with the hem of the burqa, but the woman did not move.

"You don't want that, do you?" he asked doubtfully.

At last, the woman in the burqa moved. She pulled something from under her robe. It was the baby who had started the whole terrible ordeal. Its little brown eyes were open and, for the first time, they reflected the radiant light that burned through Tim's dream like life itself. The infant struggled against its mother to stand up, sticking its thumb into its mouth. It had chubby legs, free of viscera or damage or blood that kicked against its mother's thighs. It rose on its own feet, leaned against its mother's breast and stared back at Tim.

Tim let a sad smile cross his lips as the baby stared at him with the curiosity of a healthy child learning about a new world.

He gave another sad smile and then he walked away.

OTHER BOOKS BY SASTRUGI PRESS

2024 Total Eclipse State Series by Aaron Linsdau
Sastrugi Press has published state-specific and country guides for the 2024 total eclipse crossing over North America. Check the Sastrugi Press website for the available eclipse books for Texas, Arkansas, Oklahoma, Missouri, Kentucky, Illinois, Indiana, Ohio, Pennsylvania, New York, Vermont, New Hampshire, Maine, Mexico, and Canada.
www.sastrugipress.com/eclipse

50 Wildlife Hotspots by Moose Henderson
Find out where to find animals and photograph them in Grand Teton National Park from a professional wildlife photographer. This unique guide shares the secret locations with the best chance at spotting wildlife.

A Small Pile of Feathers by Gerry Spence
Gerry Spence reveals his spiritual, loving, and sometimes humorous sides, depicted in his devotion to family and to preserving the wild places he writes of as though they were inscribed on his own bones and in his own blood.

Along the Sylvan Trail by Julianne Couch
Along the Sylvan Trail dips into the lives of linked characters as they confront futures that aren't clearly dictated by conventional planning. The conflicts of the small town change and pressure residents of Sylvan Grove to look beyond their world to the outside.

Antarctic Tears by Aaron Linsdau
What would make someone give up a high-paying career to ski alone across Antarctica to the South Pole? This inspirational true story will make readers both cheer and cry. Fighting skin-freezing temperatures, infections, and emotional breakdown, Aaron Linsdau exposes the harsh realities of the world's largest wilderness. Discover what drives someone to the brink of destruction to pursue a dream.

The Diary of a Dude Wrangler by Struthers Burt
The dude ranch world of Struthers Burt was a romantic destination in the early twentieth century. They transported people back to the Wild West. These ranches were and still are popular destinations. Experience the old west through this dude rancher's writing.

Lost at Windy Corner by Aaron Linsdau

Windy Corner on Denali has claimed lives, fingers, and toes. What would make someone brave lethal weather, crevasses, and slick ice to attempt to summit North America's highest mountain? The author shares the lessons Denali teaches on managing goals and risks. Apply the message to build resilience and overcome adversity.

Sagebrush Alley by Patricia Jones

What's worse than having a stalker? Being pursued by a second one who has already killed. Attempting to complete her studies, Dana Cameron has to avoid becoming a murder victim. She becomes tangled in a struggle for life trapped in a claustrophobic nightmare.

Sleeping Dogs Don't Lie by Michael McCoy

A young Native American boy is taken from his home after tragedy strikes, grows up in middle America, and through his first real adult summer searches for Wyoming artifacts, falls in with the subversive Dog Soldiers Resurrected, and attempts single-handedly to solve the mystery behind the murder of his treasured coworker.

So I Said by Gerry Spence

The collected sayings of Gerry Spence prods readers into thinking about their own vision of the world. As a lawyer with decades of experience in defending the defenseless, he's fought against giants. His insights provide a grander vision of how the nearly invisible world of the justice system in *So I Said*.

Voices at Twilight by Lori Howe, Ph.D.

Voices at Twilight is a guide that takes readers on a visual tour of twelve past and present Wyoming ghost towns. Contained within are travel directions, GPS coordinates, and tips for intrepid readers.www.sastrugipress.com

Do you enjoy classic literature? Sastrugi Press has a classic series just for you. Visit our webpage and find more quality books like this one at www.sastrugipress.com/classics/.

Visit Sastrugi Press on the web at www.sastrugipress.com to purchase the above titles in bulk. They are also available from your local bookstore or online retailers in print, e-book, or audiobook form. Thank you for choosing Sastrugi Press.